The Revolt of the Animals

Suddenly the barn door burst open and all hell broke loose. The pigs were in the feed bags, ripping them open, wallowing in the floury stuff. A bull ran wild, snorting and bellowing as he saw the man. Two dead sheep, trampled and ripped, lay in the yard . . . the rest must have fled in terror.

Suddenly something loomed out of the woods and mist. It was gray, enormous, reaching for the sky. The bull lifted his head, snorted. The pigs stopped their battering attack, and for a moment there was silence.

A shotgun blast ripped like thunder. The old boar was suddenly galloping in circles, wild with pain. Another explosion sent the bull crazy.

An elephant, gibbered Brock's mind, *an elephant come to help—*

The big gray shape moved slowly in on the pigs. They milled uneasily, their eyes full of hate and terror.

Then Brock looked up into the wizened brown face of a chimpanzee who was holding a shotgun . . . and he knew the world would never be the same!

BRAIN WAVE

Poul Anderson

A Del Rey Book

BALLANTINE BOOKS • NEW YORK

A Del Rey Book
Published by Ballantine Books

Library of Congress Catalog Card Number: 54-8910

ISBN 0-345-27556-X

Manufactured in the United States of America

First Edition: June 1954
Seventh Printing: July 1978

Cover art by Michael Herring

To
Karen,
of course

CHAPTER *1*

THE trap had closed at sundown. In the last red light, the rabbit had battered himself against its walls until fear and numbness ached home and he crouched shaken by the flutterings of his own heart. Otherwise there was no motion in him as night and the stars came. But when the moon rose, its light was caught icily in his great eyes, and he looked through shadows to the forest.

His vision was not made to focus closely, but after a while it fell on the entrance to the trap. It had snapped down on him when he entered, and then there had been only the flat bruising beat of himself against the wood. Now slowly, straining through the white unreal haze of moonlight, he recalled a memory of the gate falling, and he squeaked ever so faintly with terror. For the gate was there now, solid and sullen against the breathing forest, and yet it *had* been up and *had* come thunking down, and this now-then doubleness was something the rabbit had never known before.

The moon rose higher, swinging through a sky full of stars. An owl hooted, and the rabbit froze into moveless-ness as its wings ghosted overhead. There was fear and bewilderment and a new kind of pain in the owl's voice, too. Presently it was gone, and only the many little murmurs and smells of night were around him. And he sat for a long time looking at the gate and remembering how it had fallen.

The moon began to fall too, into a paling western heaven. Perhaps the rabbit wept a little, in his own way. A dawn which was as yet only a mist in the dark limned the bars of the trap against gray trees. And there was a crossbar low on the gate.

Slowly, very slowly, the rabbit inched across until he

was at the entrance. He shrank from the thing which had clamped him in. It smelled of man. Then he nosed it, feeling dew cold and wet on his muzzle. It did not stir. But it had fallen down.

The rabbit crouched, bracing his shoulders against the crossbar. He strained then, heaving upward, and the wood shivered. The rabbit's breath came fast and sharp, whistling between his teeth, and he tried again. The gate moved upward in its grooves, and the rabbit bolted free.

For an instant he poised wildly. The sinking moon was a blind dazzle in his eyes. The gate smacked back into place, and he turned and fled.

Archie Brock had been out late grubbing stumps in the north forty. Mr. Rossman wanted them all pulled by Wednesday so he could get the plowing started in his new field, and promised Brock extra pay if he would see to it. So Brock took some dinner out with him and worked till it got too dark to see. Then he started walking the three miles home, because they didn't let him use the jeep or a truck.

He was tired without thinking of it, aching a little and wishing he had a nice tall beer. But mostly he didn't think at all, just picked them up and laid them down, and the road slid away behind him. There were dark woods on either side, throwing long shadows across the moon-whitened dust, and he heard the noise of crickets chirring and once there was an owl. Have to take a gun and get that owl before he swiped some chickens. Mr. Rossman didn't mind if Brock hunted.

It was funny the way he kept thinking things tonight. Usually he just went along, especially when he was as tired as now, but—maybe it was the moon—he kept remembering bits of things, and words sort of formed themselves in his head like someone was talking. He thought about his bed and how nice it would have been to drive home from work; only of course he got sort of mixed up when driving, and there'd been a couple of smashups. Funny he should have done that, because all at once it didn't seem so hard: just a few signals to learn, and you kept your eyes open, and that was all.

2

The sound of his feet was hollow on the road. He breathed deeply, drawing a cool night into his lungs, and looked upward, away from the moon. The stars were sure big and bright tonight.

Another memory came back to him, somebody had said the stars were like the sun only further away. It hadn't made much sense then. But maybe it was so, like a light was a small thing till you got up close and then maybe it was very big. Only if the stars were as big as the sun, they'd have to be awful far away.

He stopped dead, feeling a sudden cold run through him. Jesus God! How far *up* the stars were!

The earth seemed to fall away underfoot, he was hanging on to a tiny rock that spun crazily through an everlasting darkness, and the great stars burned and roared around him, so far up that he whimpered with knowing it.

He began to run.

The boy rose early, even if it was summer and no school and breakfast wouldn't be for a while yet. The street and the town outside his windows looked very clean and bright in the young sunshine. A single truck clattered down the road and a man in blue denim walked toward the creamery carrying a lunch pail, otherwise it was as if he had the whole world to himself. His father was already off to work, and Mom liked to go back to bed for an hour after fixing his breakfast, and Sis was still asleep, so the boy was all alone in the house.

His friend was coming over and they'd go fishing, but first he wanted to get some more done on his model plane. He washed as thoroughly as you could ask a ten-year-old to, snatched a roll from the pantry, and went back to his room and the littered table there. The plane was going to be a real beauty, a Shooting Star with a CO_2 cartridge to make a jet. Only somehow, this morning it didn't look as good as it had last night. He wished he could make a real jet motor for it.

He sighed, pushing the work away, and took a sheet of paper. He'd always liked to doodle around with numbers, and one of the teachers had taught him a little about algebra. Some of the fellows had called him teacher's pet for

3

that, till he licked them, but it was real interesting, not just like learning multiplication tables. Here you made the numbers and letters do something. The teacher said that if he really wanted to build spaceships when he grew up, he'd have to learn lots of math.

He started drawing some graphs. The different kinds of equations made different pictures. It was fun to see how $x = ky + c$ made a straight line while $x^2 + y^2 = c$ was always a circle. Only how if you changed one of the x's, made it equal 3 instead of 2? What would happen to the y in the meantime? He'd never thought of that before!

He grasped the pencil tightly, his tongue sticking out of the corner of his mouth. You had to kind of sneak up on the x and the y, change one of them just a weeny little bit, and then——

He was well on the way to inventing differential calculus when his mother called him down to breakfast.

CHAPTER 2

PETER CORINTH came out of the shower, still singing vigorously, to find Sheila busy frying bacon and eggs. He ruffled her soft brown hair up, kissing her on the neck, and she turned to smile at him.

"She looks like an angel and cooks like an angel," he said.

"Why, Pete," she answered, "you never——"

"Never could find words," he agreed. "But it's gospel truth, me love." He bent over the pan, inhaling the crisp odor with a contented sigh. "I have a hunch this is one of those days when everything will go right," he said. "A bit of *Hubris* for which the gods will doubtless visit a *Nemesis* on me. *Ate:* Gertie, the slut, will burn out a tube. But you'll amend it all."

"*Hubris, Nemesis, Ate.*" A tiny frown creased her broad

4

clear forehead. "You've used those words before, Pete. What do they mean?"

He blinked at her. Two years after marriage, he was still far gone in love with his wife, and as she stood there his heart turned over within him. She was kind and merry and beautiful and she could cook—but she was nothing of an intellectual, and when his friends came over she sat quietly back, taking no part in the conversation. "What do you care?" he asked.

"I was just wondering," she said.

He went into the bedroom and began dressing, leaving the door open so he could explain the basis of Greek tragedy. It was much too bright a morning to dwell on so somber a theme, but she listened closely, with an occasional question. When he came out, she smiled and went over to him.

"You dear clumsy physicist," she said. "You're the only man I ever knew who could put on a suit straight from the cleaners and make it look like you'd been fixing a car in it." She adjusted his tie and pulled down the rumpled coat. He ran a hand through his black hair, immediately reducing it to unkemptness, and followed her to the kitchenette table. A whiff of steam from the coffeepot fogged his horn-rimmed glasses, and he took them off and polished them on his necktie. His lean, broken-nosed face looked different without them—younger, perhaps only the thirty-three years which was his actual age.

"It came to me just when I woke up," he said as he buttered his toast. "I must have a well-trained subconscious after all."

"You mean the solution to your problem?" asked Sheila.

He nodded, too absorbed to consider what her query meant. She usually just let him run on, saying "yes" and "no" in the right places but not really listening. To her, his work was altogether mysterious. He had sometimes thought she lived in a child's world, with nothing very well known but all of it bright and strange.

"I've been trying to build a phase analyzer for inter-molecular resonance bonds in crystal structure," he said. "Well, no matter. The thing is, I've been plugging along for the past few weeks, trying to design a circuit which

5

would do what I wanted, and was baffled. Then I woke up just this morning with an idea that might work. Let's see——" His eyes looked beyond her and he ate without tasting. Sheila laughed, very softly.

"I may be late tonight," he said at the door. "If this new idea of mine pans out, I may not want to break off work till— Lord knows when. I'll call you."

"Okay, honey. Good hunting."

When he was gone, Sheila stood for a moment smiling after him. Pete was a—well, she was just lucky, that was all. She'd never really appreciated how lucky, but this morning seemed different, somehow. Everything stood out sharp and clear, as if she were up in the Western mountains her husband loved so well.

She hummed to herself as she washed the dishes and straightened up the apartment. Memory slid through her, the small-town Pennsylvania girlhood, the business college, her coming to New York four years ago to take a clerical job at the office of a family acquaintance. Dear God, but she had been unsuited for that kind of life! One party and boy friend after another, everybody fast-talking, jerky-moving, carefully hard-boiled and knowing, the expensive and market-wise crowd where she always had to be on her guard—— All right, she'd married Pete on the rebound, after Bill walked out calling her a stupid—— never mind. But she'd always liked the shy, quiet man, and she had been on the rebound from a whole concept of living.

So I'm stodgy now, she told herself, *and glad of it, too.*

An ordinary housewifely existence, nothing more spectacular than a few friends in for beer and talk, going to church now and then while Pete, the agnostic, slept late; vacation trips in New England or the Rocky Mountains; plans of having a kid soon—who wanted more? Her friends before had always been ready for a good laugh at the shibboleth-ridden boredom which was bourgeois existence; but when you got right down to it, they had only traded one routine and one set of catchwords for another, and seemed to have lost something of reality into the bargain.

Sheila shook her head, puzzled. It wasn't like her to go

daydreaming this way. Her thoughts even sounded different, somehow.

She finished the housework and looked about her. Normally she relaxed for a while before lunch with one of the pocket mysteries which were her prime vice; afterward there was some shopping to do, maybe a stroll in the park, maybe a visit to or from some woman friend, and then supper to fix and Pete to expect. But today——

She picked up the detective story she had planned to read. For a moment the bright cover rested between uncertain fingers, and she almost sat down with it. Then, shaking her head, she laid it back and went over to the crowded bookshelf, took out Pete's worn copy of *Lord Jim,* and returned to the armchair. Midafternoon came before she realized that she had forgotten all about lunch.

Corinth met Felix Mandelbaum in the elevator going down. They were that rare combination, neighbors in a New York apartment building who had become close friends. Sheila, with her small-town background, had insisted on getting to know everyone on their own floor at least, and Corinth had been glad of it in the case of the Mandelbaums. Sarah was a plump, quiet, retiring *Hausfrau* sort, pleasant but not colorful; her husband was a horse of quite another shade.

Felix Mandelbaum had been born fifty years ago in the noise and dirt and sweatshops of the lower East Side, and life had been kicking him around ever since; but he kicked back, with a huge enjoyment. He'd been everything from itinerant fruit picker to skilled machinist and O.S.S. operative overseas during the war—where his talent for languages and people must have come in handy. His career as a labor organizer ran parallel, from the old Wobblies to the comparative respectability of his present job: officially executive secretary of a local union, actually a roving trouble shooter with considerable voice in national councils. Not that he had been a radical since his twenties; he said he'd seen radicalism from the inside, and that was enough for any sane man. Indeed, he claimed to be one of the last true conservatives—only, to conserve, you had to prune and graft and adjust. He was self-educated, but

7

widely read, with more capacity for life than anyone else of Corinth's circle except possibly Nat Lewis. Fun to know.

"Hello," said the physicist. "You're late today."

"Not exactly." Mandelbaum's voice was a harsh New York tone, fast and clipped. He was a small, wiry, gray-haired man, with a gnarled beaky face and intense dark eyes. "I woke up with an idea. A reorganization plan. Amazing nobody's thought of it yet. It'd halve the paper work. So I've been outlining a chart."

Corinth shook his head dolefully. "By now, Felix, you should know that Americans are too fond of paper work to give up one sheet," he said.

"You haven't seen Europeans," grunted Mandelbaum.

"You know," said Corinth, "it's funny you should've had your idea just today. (Remind me to get the details from you later, it sounds interesting.) I woke up with the solution to a problem that's been bedeviling me for the past month."

"Hm?" Mandelbaum pounced on the fact, you could almost see him turning it over in his hands, sniffing it, and laying it aside. "Odd." It was a dismissal.

The elevator stopped and they parted company. Corinth took the subway as usual. He was currently between cars; in this town, it just didn't pay to own one. He noticed vaguely that the train was quieter than ordinarily. People were less hurried and unmannerly, they seemed thoughtful. He glanced at the newspapers, wondering with a gulp if *it* had started, but there was nothing really sensational—except maybe for that local bit about a dog, kept overnight in a basement, which had somehow opened the deep freeze, dragged out the meat to thaw, and been found happily gorged. Otherwise: fighting here and there throughout the world, a strike, a Communist demonstration in Rome, four killed in an auto crash—words, as if rotary presses squeezed the blood from everything that went through them.

Emerging in lower Manhattan, he walked three blocks to the Rossman Institute, limping a trifle. The same accident which had broken his nose years ago had injured his right knee and kept him out of military service; though being yanked directly from his youthful college graduation

8

into the Manhattan Project might have had something to do with that.

He winced at the trailing memory. Hiroshima and Nagasaki still lay heavily on his conscience. He had quit immediately after the war, and it was not only to resume his studies or to escape the red tape and probing and petty intrigue of government research for the underpaid sanity of academic life; it had been a flight from guilt. So had his later activities, he supposed—the Atomic Scientists, the United World Federalists, the Progressive Party. When he thought how those had withered away or been betrayed, and recalled the brave clichés which had stood like a shield between him and the Soviet snarl—there for any to see who had eyes—he wondered how sane the professors were after all.

Only, was his present retreat into pure research and political passivity—voting a discouraged Democratic ticket and doing nothing else—any more balanced? Nathan Lewis, frankly labeling himself a reactionary, was a local Republican committeeman, an utter and cheerful pessimist who still tried to salvage something; and Felix Mandelbaum, no less realistic than his chess and bull-session opponent Lewis, had more hope and energy, even looked forward to the ultimate creation of a genuine American Labor Party. Between them, Corinth felt rather pallid.

And I'm younger than either one!

He sighed. What was the matter with him? Thoughts kept boiling up out of nowhere, forgotten things, linking themselves into new chains that rattled in his skull. And just when he had the answer to his problem, too.

That reflection drove all others out. Again, it was unusual: ordinarily he was slow to change any train of thought. He stepped forward with a renewed briskness.

The Rossman Institute was a bulk of stone and glass, filling half a block and looking almost shiny among its older neighbors. It was known as a scientist's heaven. Able men from all places and all disciplines were drawn there, less by the good pay than by the chance to do unhampered research of their own choosing, with first-rate equipment and none of the projectitis which was strangling pure science in government, in industry, and in too many universities. It had the inevitable politicking and backbiting, but in lesser degree than the average college; it was the Institute for Advanced Study—less abstruse and more energetic, perhaps, and certainly with much more room. Lewis had once cited it to Mandelbaum as proof of the cultural necessity for a privileged class. "D'you think any government would ever endow such a thing and then, what's more, have the sense to leave it to itself?"

"Brookhaven does all right," Mandelbaum had said, but for him it was a feeble answer.

Corinth nodded to the girl at the newsstand in the lobby, hailed a couple of acquaintances, and fumed at the slowness of the elevator. "Seventh," he said automatically when it arrived.

"I should know that, Dr. Corinth," grinned the operator. "You've been here—let's see—almost six years now, isn't it?"

The physicist blinked. The attendant had always been part of the machinery to him; they had exchanged the usual pleasantries, but it hadn't meant a thing. Suddenly Corinth saw him as a human being, a living and unique organism, part of an enormous impersonal web which ultimately became the entire universe, and yet bearing his own heart within him. *Now why,* he asked himself amazedly, *should I think that?*

"You know, sir," said the attendant, "I been wondering. I woke up this morning and wondered what I was doing this for and if I really wanted more out of it than just my job and my pension and——" He paused awkwardly as they stopped to let off a third-floor passenger. "I envy you. You're going somewhere."

The elevator reached the seventh floor. "You could—well, you could take a night course if you wanted," said Corinth.

"I think maybe I will, sir. If you'd be so kind as to recommend—— Well, later. I got to go now." The doors slid smoothly across the cage, and Corinth went down hard marble ways to his laboratory.

He had a permanent staff of two, Johansson and Grunewald, intense young men who probably dreamed of having labs of their own someday. They were already there when he entered and took off his coat.

"Good morning . . . 'Morning . . . 'Morning."

"I've been thinking, Pete," said Grunewald suddenly, as the chief went over to his desk. "I've got an idea for a circuit that may work——"

"*Et tu, Brute*," murmured Corinth. He sat down on a stool, doubling his long legs under him. "Let's have it."

Grunewald's gimmick seemed remarkably parallel to his own. Johansson, usually silent and competent and no more, chimed in eagerly as thoughts occurred to him. Corinth took over leadership in the discussion, and within half an hour they were covering paper with the esoteric symbols of electronics.

Rossman might not have been entirely disinterested in establishing the Institute, though a man with his bank account could afford altruism. Pure research helped industry. He had made his fortune in light metals, all the way from raw ores to finished products, with cross-connections to a dozen other businesses; officially semi-retired, he kept his fine thin hands on the strings. Even bacteriology could turn out to be useful—not very long ago, work had been done on bacterial extraction of oil from shales—and Corinth's study of crystal bonds could mean a good deal to metallurgy. Grunewald fairly gloated over the prospect of what success would do to their professional reputations. Before noon, they had set up a series of partial differential equations which would go to the computer at their regular scheduled time to use it, and were drawing up elements of the circuit they wanted.

The phone rang. It was Lewis, suggesting lunch together. "I'm on a hot trail today," said Corinth. "I thought maybe I'd just have some sandwiches sent up."

"Well, either I am too, or else I'm up you know what creek with no paddle," said Lewis. "I'm not sure which, and it might help me straighten out my ideas if I could bounce them off you."

"Oh, all right. Commissary do?"

"If you merely want to fill your belly, I suppose so." Lewis went in for three-hour lunches complete with wine and violins, a habit he had picked up during his years in

11

pre-Anschluss Vienna. "One o'clock suit you? The peasantry will have gorged by then."

"Okay." Corinth hung up and lost himself again in the cool ecstasy of his work. It was one-thirty before he noticed the time, and he hurried off swearing.

Lewis was just seating himself at a table when Corinth brought his tray over. "I figured from your way of talk you'd be late," he said. "What'd you get? The usual cafeteria menu, I suppose: mice drowned in skim milk, fillet of sea urchin, baked chef's special, baked chef—well, no matter." He sipped his coffee and winced.

He didn't look delicate: a short square man of forty-eight, getting a little plump and bald, sharp eyes behind thick, rimless glasses. He was, indeed, a hearty soul at table or saloon. But eight years in Europe did change tastes, and he insisted that his postwar visits had been purely gastronomical.

"What you need," said Corinth with the smugness of a convert, "is to get married."

"I used to think so, when I began leaving my libertine days behind. But, well, never mind. Too late now." Lewis attacked a minute steak, which he always pronounced as if the adjective were synonymous with "tiny," and scowled through a mouthful. "I'm more interested in the histological aspect of biology just now."

"You said you were having trouble——"

"That's mostly with my assistants. Everybody seems jumpy today, and young Roberts is coming up with even wilder ideas than usual. But it's my work. I've told you, haven't I? I'm studying nerve cells—neurones. Trying to keep them alive in different artificial media, and seeing how their electrical properties vary with conditions. I have them in excised sections of tissue—Lindbergh-Carrel technique, with modifications. It was coming along pretty good —and then today, when we ran a routine check, the results came out different. So I tested them all——Every one is changed!"

"Hm?" Corinth raised his eyebrows and chewed quietly for a minute. "Something wrong with your apparatus?"

"Not that I can find. Nothing different—except the cells themselves. A small but significant shift." Lewis' tones came

12

faster, with a hint of rising excitement. "You know how a neurone works? Like a digital computer. It's stimulated by a—a stimulus, fires a signal, and is thereafter inactive for a short time. The next neurone in the nerve gets the signal, fires, and is also briefly inactivated. Well, it turns out that everything is screwy today. The inactivation time is a good many microseconds less, the—well, let's just say the whole system reacts significantly faster than normally. And the signals are also more intense."

Corinth digested the information briefly, then, slowly: "Looks like you may have stumbled onto something big."

"Well, where's the cause? The medium, the apparatus, it's all the same as yesterday, I tell you. I'm going nuts trying to find out if I've got a potential Nobel Prize or just sloppy technique!"

Very slowly, as if his mind were shying away from a dimly seen realization, Corinth said: "It's odd this should have happened today."

"Hm?" Lewis glanced sharply up, and Corinth related his own encounters.

"Very odd," agreed the biologist. "And no big thunderstorms lately—ozone stimulates the mind—but my cultures are sealed in glass anyway——" Something flashed in his eyes.

Corinth looked around. "Hullo, there's Helga. Wonder what made her so late? Hi, there!" He stood up, waving across the room, and Helga Arnulfsen bore her tray over to their table and sat down.

She was a tall, rangy, handsome woman, her long blonde hair drawn tightly around the poised head, but something in her manner—an impersonal energy, an aloofness, perhaps only the unfeminine crispness of speech and dress— made her less attractive than she could have been. She'd changed since the old days, right after the war, thought Corinth. He'd been taking his doctorate at Minnesota, where she was studying journalism, and they'd had fun together; though he'd been too much and too hopelessly in love with his work and another girl to think seriously about her. Afterward they had corresponded, and he had gotten her a secretarial post at the Institute, two years

13

before. She was chief administrative assistant now, and did a good job of it.

"Whew! What a day!" She ran a strong slim hand across her hair, sleeking it down, and smiled wearily at them. "Everybody and his Uncle Oscar is having trouble, and all of them are wishing it on me. Gertie threw a tantrum——"

"Huh?" Corinth regarded her in some dismay. He'd been counting on the big computer to solve his equations that day. "What's wrong?"

"Only God and Gertie know, and neither one is telling. Allanbee ran a routine test this morning, and it came out wrong. Not much, but enough to throw off anybody that needed precise answers. He's been digging into her ever since, trying to find the trouble, so far without luck. And I have to reschedule everybody!"

"Very strange," murmured Lewis.

"Then different instruments, especially in the physics and chemistry sections, are a little crazy. Murchison's polarimeter has an error of—oh, something horrible like one tenth of one per cent, I don't know."

"Izzat so?" Lewis leaned forward, thrusting his jaw out above the dishes. "Maybe it's not my neurones but my instruments that're off whack—— No, can't be. Not that much. It must be something in the cells themselves—but how can I measure that if the gadgets are all awry?" He broke into vigorous German profanity, though his eyes remained alight.

"Lots of the boys have come up with brave new projects all at once, too," went on Helga. "They want immediate use of things like the big centrifuge, and blow their tops when I tell them to wait their turn."

"All today, eh?" Corinth pushed his dessert aside and took out a cigarette. " 'Curiouser and curiouser,' said Alice." His eyes widened, and the hand that struck a match shook ever so faintly. "Nat, I wonder——"

"A general phenomenon?" Lewis nodded, holding excitement in check with an effort. "Could be, could be. We'd certainly better find out."

"What're you talking about?" asked Helga.

"Things." Corinth explained while she finished eating.

14

Lewis sat quietly back, blowing cigar fumes and withdrawn into himself.

"Hm." Helga tapped the table with a long, unpainted fingernail. "Sounds—interesting. Are all nerve cells, including those in our own brains, suddenly being speeded up?"

"It's more basic than that," said Corinth. "Something may have happened to—what? Electrochemical phenomena? How should I know? Let's not go off the deep end till we've investigated this."

"Yeah. I'll leave it to you." Helga took out a cigarette for herself and inhaled deeply. "I can think of a few obvious things to check up on—but it's your child." She turned again to smile at Corinth, the gentle smile she saved for a very few. "Apropos, how's Sheila?"

"Oh, fine, fine. How's yourself?"

"I'm okay." There was a listlessness in her answer.

"You must come over to our place sometime for dinner." It was a small strain to carry on polite conversation, when his mind was yelling to be at this new problem. "We haven't seen you in quite a while. Bring the new boy friend if you want, whoever he is."

"Jim? Oh, him. I gave him the sack last week. But I'll come over, sure." She got up. "Back to the oars, mates. See you."

Corinth regarded her as she strode toward the cashier's desk. Almost in spite of himself—his thoughts were shooting off in all directions today—he murmured: "I wonder why she can't keep a man. She's good-looking and intelligent enough."

"She doesn't want to," said Lewis shortly.

"No, I suppose not. She's turned cold since I knew her in Minneapolis. Why?"

Lewis shrugged.

"I think you know," said Corinth. "You've always understood women better than you had any right to. And she likes you better than anyone else around here, I think."

"We both go for music," said Lewis. It was his opinion that none had been written since 1900. "And we both know how to keep our mouths shut."

"Okay, okay," laughed Corinth. He got up. "I'm for

15

the lab again. Hate to scrap the phase analyzer, but this new business——" Pausing: "Look, let's get hold of the others and divide up the labor, huh? Everybody check something. It won't take long then."

Lewis nodded curtly and followed him out.

By evening the results were in. As Corinth looked at the figures, his interest lost way to a coldness rising within him. He felt suddenly how small and helpless a thing he was.

Electromagnetic phenomena were changed.

It wasn't much, but the very fact that the supposedly eternal constants of nature had shifted was enough to crash a hundred philosophies into dust. The subtlety of the problem held something elemental. How do you remeasure the basic factors when your measuring devices have themselves changed?

Well, there were ways. There are no absolutes in this universe, everything exists in relation to everything else, and it was the fact that certain data had altered relatively to others which was significant.

Corinth had been working on the determination of electrical constants. For the metals they were the same, or nearly the same, as before, but the resistivity and permittivity of insulators had changed measurably—they had become slightly better conductors.

Except in the precision apparatus, such as Gertie the computer, the change in electromagnetic characteristics was not enough to make any noticeable difference. But the most complex and delicately balanced mechanism known to man is the living cell; and the neurone is the most highly evolved and specialized of all cells—particularly that variety of neurones found in the human cerebral cortex. And here the change was felt. The minute electrical impulses which represented neural functioning—sense awareness, motor reaction, thought itself—were flowing more rapidly, more intensely.

And the change might just have begun.

Helga shivered. "I need a drink," she said. "Bad."

"I know a bar," said Lewis. "I'll join you in one before coming back to work some more. How about you, Pete?"

"I'm going home," said the physicist. "Have fun." His words were flat.

He walked out, hardly aware of the darkened lobby and the late hour. To the others, this was still something bright and new and wonderful; but he couldn't keep from thinking that perhaps, in one huge careless swipe, the universe was about to snuff out all the race of man. What would the effect be on a living body——?

Well, they'd done about all they could for now. They'd checked as much as possible. Helga had gotten in touch with the Bureau of Standards in Washington and notified them. She gathered, from what the man there said, that a few other laboratories, spotted throughout the country, had also reported anomalies. *Tomorrow,* thought Corinth, *they'll really start hearing about it.*

Outside—the scene was still New York at evening—hardly changed, perhaps just a little quieter than it should be. He bought a newspaper at the corner and glanced at it as he stood there. Was he wrong, or had a subtle difference crept in, a more literate phrasing, something individual that broke through the copyreader's barriers because the copyreader himself had changed without knowing it? But there was no mention of the great cause, that was too big and too new yet, nor had the old story altered—war, unrest, suspicion, fear and hate and greed, a sick world crumbling.

He was suddenly aware that he had read through the *Times'* crowded front page in about ten minutes. He shoved the newspaper into a pocket and hastened toward the subway.

17

CHAPTER *3*

THERE was trouble everywhere. An indignant yell in the morning brought Archie Brock running to the chicken house, where Stan Wilmer had set down a bucket of feed to shake his fist at the world.

"Look a' that!" he cried. "Just look!"

Brock craned his neck through the door and whistled. The place was a mess. A couple of bloody-feathered corpses were sprawled on the straw, a few other hens cackled nervously on the roosts, and that was all. The rest were gone.

"Looks like foxes got in when somebody left the door open," said Brock.

"Yeah." Wilmer swallowed his rage in a noisy gulp. "Some stinking son of a——"

Brock remembered that Wilmer was in charge of the hen house, but decided not to mention it. The other man recalled it himself and paused, scowling.

"I don't know," he said slowly. "I checked the place last night as usual, before going to bed, and I'll swear the door was closed and hooked like it always is. Five years I been here and never had any trouble."

"So maybe somebody opened the door later on, after dark, huh?"

"Yeah. A chicken thief. Though it's funny the dogs didn't bark—I never heard of any human being coming here without them yapping." Wilmer shrugged bitterly. "Well, anyway, somebody did open the door."

"And then later on foxes got in." Brock turned one of the dead hens over with his toe. "And maybe had to run for it when one of the dogs came sniffing around, and left these."

"And most of the birds wandered out into the woods.

18

It'll take a week to catch 'em—all that live. Oh, Judas!" Wilmer stormed out of the chicken house, forgetting to close the door. Brock did it for him, vaguely surprised that he had remembered to do so.

He sighed and resumed his morning chores. The animals all seemed fidgety today. And damn if his own head didn't feel funny. He remembered his own panic of two nights before, and the odd way he'd been thinking ever since. Maybe there was some kind of fever going around.

Well—he'd ask somebody about it later. There was work to do today, plowing in the north forty that had just been cleared. All the tractors were busy cultivating, so he'd have to take a team of horses.

That was all right. Brock liked animals, he had always understood them and got along with them better than with people. Not that the people had been mean to him, anyway for a long while now. The kids used to tease him, back when he was a kid too, and then later there'd been some trouble with cars, and a couple of girls had got scared also and he'd been beaten up by the brother of one of them. But that was years back. Mr. Rossman had told him carefully what he could do and could not do, kind of taken him over, and things had been all right since then. Now he could walk into the tavern when he was in town and have a beer like anybody else, and the men said hello.

He stood for a minute, wondering why he should be thinking about this when he knew it so well, and why it should hurt him the way it did. *I'm all right,* he thought. *I'm not so smart, maybe, but I'm strong. Mr. Rossman says he ain't got a better farm hand nor me.*

He shrugged and entered the barn to get out the horses. He was a young man, of medium height but heavy-set and muscular, with coarse strong features and a round, crew-cut, red-haired head. His blue denim clothes were shabby but clean; Mrs. Bergen, the wife of the general superintendent in whose cottage he had a room, looked after such details for him.

The barn was big and gloomy, full of the strong rich smells of hay and horses. The brawny Percherons stamped and snorted, restless as he harnessed them. Funny—they were always so calm before. "So, so, steady, boy. Steady,

19

Tom. Whoa, there, Jerry. Easy, easy." They quieted a little and he led them out and hitched them to a post while he went into the shed after the plow.

His dog Joe came frisking around him, a tall Irish setter whose coat was like gold and copper in the sun. Joe was really Mr. Rossman's, of course, but Brock had taken care of him since he was a pup and it was always Brock whom he followed and loved. "Down, boy, down. What the hell's got into yuh, anyway? Take it easy, will yuh?"

The estate lay green around him, the farm buildings on one side, the cottages of the help screened off by trees on another, the many acres of woods behind. There was a lot of lawn and orchard and garden between this farming part and the big white house of the owner, a house which had been mostly empty since Mr. Rossman's daughters had married and his wife had died. He was there now, though, spending a few weeks here in upper New York State with his flowers. Brock wondered why a millionaire like Mr. Rossman wanted to putter around growing roses, even if he was getting old.

The shed door creaked open and Brock went in and took the big plow and wheeled it out, grunting a little with the effort. Not many men could drag it out themselves, he thought with a flicker of pride. He chuckled as he saw how the horses stamped at the sight. Horses were lazy beasts, they'd never work if they could get out of it.

He shoved the plow around behind them, carried the tongue forward, and hitched it on. With a deft motion, he twirled the reins loose from the post, took his seat, and shook the lines across the broad rumps. "Giddap!"

They just stood, moving their feet.

"Giddap there, I say!"

Tom began backing. "Whoa! Whoa!" Brock took the loose end of the reins and snapped it with whistling force. Tom grunted and put one huge hoof on the tongue. It broke across.

For a long moment, Brock sat there, finding no words. Then he shook his red head. "It's a ac-ci-dent," he said aloud. The morning seemed very quiet all of a sudden. "It's a ac-ci-dent."

There was a spare tongue in the shed. He fetched it and

some tools, and began doggedly removing the broken one.

"Hi, there! Stop! Stop, I say!"

Brock looked up. The squealing and grunting were like a blow. He saw a black streak go by, and then another and another—The pigs were loose!

"Joe!" he yelled, even then wondering a little at how quickly he reacted. "Go get 'em, Joe! Round 'em up, boy!"

The dog was off like burnished lightning. He got ahead of the lead sow and snapped at her. She grunted, turning aside, and he darted after the next. Stan Wilmer came running from the direction of the pen. His face was white.

Brock ran to intercept another pig, turning it, but a fourth one slipped aside and was lost in the woods. It took several confused minutes to chase the majority back into the pen; a number were gone.

Wilmer stood gasping. His voice was raw. "I saw it," he groaned. "Oh, my God, I saw it. It ain't possible."

Brock blew out his cheeks and wiped his face.

"You hear me?" Wilmer grasped his arm. "I saw it, I tell you, I saw it with my own eyes. Those pigs opened the gate themselves."

"Naw!" Brock felt his mouth falling open.

"I tell you, I saw it! One of 'em stood up on her hind legs and nosed the latch up. She did it all by herself. And the others were crowding right behind her. Oh, no, no, no!"

Joe came out of the woods, driving a pig before him with sardonic barks. She seemed to give up after a minute and trotted quietly toward the pen. Wilmer turned like a machine and opened the gate again and let her go in.

"Good boy!" Brock patted the silken head that nuzzled against him. "Smart dog!"

"Too God damned smart." Wilmer narrowed his eyes. "Did a dog ever make like that before?"

"Sure," said Brock uncertainly.

Joe got off his haunches and went back into the woods.

"I'll bet he's going after another pig." There was a kind of horror in Wilmer's voice.

"Sure. He's a smart dog, he is."

"I'm going to see Bill Bergen about this." Wilmer turned on his heel. Brock looked after him, shrugged heavy shoulders, and went back to his own task. By the time he finished it, Joe had rounded up two more pigs and brought them back, and was mounting guard at the gate of the pen.

"Good fellow," said Brock. "I'll see yuh get a bone for this." He hitched Tom and Jerry, who had been standing at their ease. "All right, yuh bums, let's go. Giddap!"

Slowly, the horses backed. "Hey!" screamed Brock.

This time they didn't stop with the tongue. Very carefully, they walked onto the plow itself and bent its iron frame with their weight and broke off the coulter. Brock felt his throat dry.

"No," he mumbled.

Wilmer nearly had a fit when he learned about the horses. Bergen only stood there, whistling tunelessly. "I don't know." He scratched his sandy head. "Tell you what. We'll call off all work having to do with animals, except feeding and milking, of course. Padlock every gate and have somebody check all our fence lines. I'll see the old man about this."

"Me, I'm gonna carry a gun," said Wilmer.

"Well, it might not be a bad idea," said Bergen.

Archie Brock was assigned to look at one section, a four-mile line enclosing the woods. He took Joe, who gamboled merrily in his wake, and went off glad to be alone for a change.

How still the forest was! Sunlight slanted down through green unstirring leaves, throwing a dapple on the warm brown shadows. The sky was utterly blue overhead, no clouds, no wind. His feet scrunched dully on an occasional clod or stone, he brushed against a twig and it scratched very faintly along his clothes, otherwise the land was altogether silent. The birds seemed to have quieted down all at once, no squirrels were in sight, even the sheep had withdrawn into the inner woods. He thought uneasily that somehow the whole green world had a waiting feel to it.

Like before a storm, maybe?

He could see how people would be scared if the animals started getting smarter. If they were really smart, would they keep on letting humans lock them up and work them and castrate them and kill and skin and eat them? Suppose

Tom and Jerry, now—— But they were so gentle!

And—wait—weren't the people getting smarter too? It seemed like in the last couple of days they'd been talking more, and it wasn't all about the weather and the neighbors either, it was about things like who was going to win the next election and why a rear-engine drive was better in a car. They'd always talked like that now and then, sure, but not so much, and they hadn't had so much to say, either. Even Mrs. Bergen, he'd seen her reading a magazine, and all she ever did before in her spare time was watch TV.

I'm getting smarter too!

The knowledge was like a thunderclap. He stood there for a long while, not moving, and Joe came up and sniffed his hand in a puzzled way.

I'm getting smarter.

Sure—it had to be. The way he'd been wondering lately, and remembering things, and speaking out when he'd never said anything much before—what else could it be? All the world was getting smarter.

I can read, he told himself. *Not very good, but they did teach me the al-pha-bet, and I can read a comic book. Maybe I can read a real book now.*

Books had the answers to what he was suddenly wondering about, things like the sun and moon and stars, why there was winter and summer, why they had wars and Presidents and who lived on the other side of the world and——

He shook his head, unable to grasp the wilderness that rose up inside him and spread till it covered creation further than he could see. He'd never wondered before. Things just happened and were forgotten again. *But*—He looked at his hands, marveling. *Who am I? What am I doing here?*

There was a boiling in him. He leaned his head against the cool trunk of a tree, listening to the blood roar in his ears. *Please, God, let it be real. Please make me like other people.*

After a while he fought it down and went on, checking the fence as he had been told.

In the evening, after chores, he put on a clean suit and went up to the big house. Mr. Rossman was sitting on the porch, smoking a pipe and turning the pages of a book over in his thin fingers, not really seeing it. Brock paused timidly, cap in hand, till the owner looked up and spied him.

"Oh, hello, Archie," he said in his soft voice. "How are you tonight?"

"I'm all right, thank you." Brock twisted the cap between his stumpy hands and shifted from one foot to another. "Please, can I see you for a minute?"

"Why, of course. Come on in." Mr. Rossman laid his book aside and sat smoking while Brock opened the screen door and walked over to him. "Here, take a chair."

"That's all right, thanks. I——" Brock ran his tongue across dry lips. "I'd just like to ask you 'bout something."

"Ask away, Archie." Mr. Rossman leaned back. He was a tall spare man, his face thinly carved, proud under its kindness of the moment, his hair white. Brock's parents had been tenants of his, and when it became plain that their son would never amount to anything, he had taken charge of the boy. "Everything okay?"

"Well, it's about, uh, about this change here."

"Eh?" Rossman's gaze sharpened. "What change?"

"You know. The animals getting smart and uppity."

"Oh, yes. That." Rossman blew a cloud of smoke. "Tell me, Archie, have you noticed any change in yourself?"

"Yes, I, uh, well, I think maybe I have."

Rossman nodded. "You wouldn't have come here if you hadn't changed."

"What's happening, Mr. Rossman? What's gone wrong?"

"I don't know, Archie. Nobody knows." The old man looked out into a gathering blue twilight. "Are you so sure it's wrong, though? Maybe something is finally going right."

"You don't know——"

"No. Nobody knows." Rossman's pale blue-veined hand slapped the newspaper on the table beside him. "There are hints here. The knowledge is creeping out. I'm sure much more is known, but the government has suppressed the information for fear of a panic." He grinned with a certain viciousness. "As if a world-wide phenomenon could be kept secret! But they'll hang on to their stupidity to the very end in Washington."

24

"But, Mr. Rossman——" Brock lifted his hands and let them fall again. "What can we do?"

"Wait. Wait and see. I'm going to the city soon, to find out for myself—those pet brains of mine at the Institute should——"

"You're leaving?"

Rossman shook his head, smiling. "Poor Archie. There's a horror in being helpless, isn't there? I sometimes think that's why men fear death—not because of oblivion, but because it's foredoomed, there's nothing they can do to stop it. Even fatalism is a refuge from that, in a way—— But I digress, don't I?"

He sat smoking for a long while. The summer dusk chirred and murmured around them. "Yes," he said at last, "I feel it in myself too. And it's not altogether pleasant. Not just the nervousness and the nightmares—that's merely physiological, I suppose—but the thoughts. I've always imagined myself as a quick, capable, logical thinker. Now something is coming to life within me that I don't understand at all. Sometimes my whole life seems to have been a petty and meaningless scramble. And yet I thought I'd served my family and my country well." He smiled once more. "I do hope I'll see the end of this, though. It should be interesting!"

Tears stung Brock's eyes. "What can I do?"

"Do? Live. Live from day to day. What else can a man do?" Rossman got up and put his hand on Brock's shoulder. "But keep on thinking. Keep your thinking close to the ground, where it belongs. Don't ever trade your liberty for another man's offer to do your thinking and make your mistakes for you. I had to play the feudal lord with you, Archie, but it may be that that's no longer necessary."

Brock didn't understand most of it. But it seemed Mr. Rossman was telling him to be cheerful, that this wasn't such a bad thing after all. "I though maybe I could borrow some books," he said humbly. "I'd like to see if I can read them now."

"Why, of course, Archie. Come on into the library. I'll see if I can find something suitable for you to begin on——"

CHAPTER 4

Selections from the New York *Times*, June 23:

PRESIDENT DENIES DANGER IN BRAIN SPEEDUP

'Keep Cool, Stay on Job,' Advises White House—No Harm To Humans in Change

U. S. Scientists Working On Problem—Expect Answer Soon

FALLING STOCK MARKET WORRIES WALL STREET

Declining Sales Bring Down Stock Market and Prices

U. S. in Danger of Recession, Says Economist

CHINESE TROOPS MUTINY

Communist Government Declares Emergency

NEW RELIGION FOUNDED IN LOS ANGELES

Sawyer Proclaims Self 'The Third Ba'al' —Thousands Attend Mass Meeting

FESSENDEN CALLS FOR WORLD GOVERNMENT

Iowa Isolationist Reverses Stand in Senate Speech

JOHNSON SAYS WORLD GOVERNMENT IMPRACTICAL AT PRESENT TIME

Oregon Senator Reverses Former Stand

26

Conference.

Everybody was working late, and it was ten o'clock before the meeting which Corinth had invited to his place was ready. Sheila had insisted on putting out her usual buffet of sandwiches and coffee; afterward she sat in a corner, talking quietly with Sarah Mandelbaum. Their eyes strayed occasionally to their husbands, who were playing chess, and there was a creeping fear in the gaze.

Corinth was playing better than he had ever done before. Usually he and Mandelbaum were pretty evenly matched, the physicist's slow careful strategy offsetting the unionist's nerve-racking bravura. But tonight the younger man was too distracted. He made schemes that would have delighted Capablanca, but Mandelbaum saw through them and slashed barbarically past his defenses. Corinth sighed at last and leaned back.

"I resign," he said. "It'd be mate in, uh, seven moves."

"Not so." Mandelbaum pointed a gnarled finger at king's bishop. "If you moved him over here, and then——"

"Oh, yes, you're right. No matter. I'm just not in the mood. What's keeping Nat?"

"He'll be along. Take it easy." Mandelbaum removed himself to an armchair and began stuffing a big-bowled pipe.

"I don't see how you can sit there like that when——"

"When a world's falling to pieces around my ears? Look, Pete, it's been falling apart as long as I can remember. So far, in this particular episode, no guns have come out."

"They may do so yet." Corinth got up and stood looking out the window, hands crossed behind his back and shoulders slumped. The restless glimmer of city light etched him against darkness. "Don't you see, Felix, this new factor—if we survive it at all—changes the whole basis of human life? Our society was built by and for one sort of man. Now man himself is becoming something else."

"I doubt it." The noise of a match, struck against Man-

27

delbaum's shoe, was startlingly loud. "We're still the same old animal."

"What was your I.Q. before the change?"

"I don't know."

"Never took a test?"

"Oh, sure, they made me take one now and then, to get this or that job, but I never asked for the result. What's I.Q. except the score on an I.Q. test?"

"It's more than that. It measures the ability to handle data, grasp and create abstractions——"

"*If* you're a Caucasian of West European-American cultural background. That's who the test was designed for, Pete. A Kalahari bushman would laugh if he knew it omitted water-finding ability. That's more important to him than the ability to juggle numbers. Me, I don't underrate the logic and visualization aspect of personality, but I don't have your touching faith in it, either. There's more to a man than that, and a garage mechanic may be a better survivor type than a mathematician."

"Survivor—under what conditions?"

"Any conditions. Adaptability, toughness, quickness—those are the things that count most."

"I think kindness means a lot," said Sheila timidly.

"It's a luxury, I'm afraid, though of course it's such luxuries that make us human," said Mandelbaum. "Kindness to whom? Sometimes you just have to cut loose and get violent. Some wars are necessary."

"They wouldn't be, if people had more intelligence," said Corinth. "We needn't have fought World War II if Hitler had been stopped when he entered the Rhineland. One division could have bowled him over. But the politicians were too stupid to foresee——"

"No," said Mandelbaum. "It's just that there were reasons why it wasn't—convenient, shall we say?—to call up that division. And ninety-nine per cent of the human race, no matter how smart they are, will do the convenient thing instead of the wise thing, and kid themselves into thinking they can somehow escape the consequences. We're just built that way. And then, the world is so full of old hate and superstition, and so many people are nice and tolerant and practical about it, that it's a wonder hell hasn't boiled

28

over more often throughout history." Bitterness edged his voice. "Maybe the practical people, the ones who adapt, are right after all. Maybe the most moral thing really is to put 'myself, my wife, and my little Hassan with the bandy legs' first. Like one of my sons has done. He's in Chicago now. Changed his name and had his nose bobbed. He's not ashamed of his parents, no, but he's saved himself and his family a lot of trouble and humiliation. And I honestly don't know whether to admire him for tough-minded adaptability, or call him a spineless whelp."

"We're getting rather far from the point," said Corinth, embarrassed. "What we want to do tonight is try and estimate what we, the whole world, are in for." He shook his head. "My I.Q. has gone from its former 160 to about 200 in a week. I'm thinking things that never occurred to me before. My former professional problems are becoming ridiculously easy. Only, everything else is confused. My mind keeps wandering off into the most fantastic trains of thought, some of them pretty wild and morbid. I'm nervous as a kitten, jump at shadows, afraid for no good reason at all. Now and then I get flashes where everything seems grotesque—like in a nightmare."

"You're not adjusted to your new brain yet, that's all," said Sarah.

"I feel the same sort of things Pete does," said Sheila. Her voice was thin and scared. "It isn't worth it."

The other woman shrugged, spreading her hands. "Me, I thing it's kind of fun."

"Matter of basic personality—which has not changed," said Mandelbaum. "Sarah's always been a pretty down-to-earth sort. You just don't take your new mind seriously, Liebchen. To you, the power of abstract thought is a toy. It's got little to do with the serious matters of housework." He puffed, meshing his face into wrinkles as he squinted through the smoke. "And me, I get crazy spells like you do, Pete, but I don't let it bother me. It's only physio-logical, and I haven't time for such fumblydiddles. Not the way things are now. Everybody in the union seems to have come up with some crank notion of how we ought to run things. A guy in the electrical workers has a notion that the electricians ought to go on strike and take over the

29

whole government! Somebody even fired a shotgun at me the other day."

"Huh?" They stared at him.

Mandelbaum shrugged. "He was a lousy shot. But some people are turning crank, and some are turning mean, and most are just plain scared. Those like me who're trying to ride out the storm and keep things as nearly normal as possible, are bound to make enemies. People think a lot more today, but they aren't thinking straight."

"Sure," said Corinth. "The average man——" He started as the doorbell rang. "That must be them now," he said. "Come in."

Helga Arnulfsen entered, her slim height briefly concealing Nathan Lewis' bulk. She looked as cool and smooth and hard as before, but there were shadows under her eyes. "Hullo," she said tonelessly.

"No fun, huh?" asked Sheila with sympathy.

Helga grimaced. "Nightmares."

"Me too." A shudder ran along Sheila's small form.

"How about the psych man you were going to bring, Nat?" asked Corinth.

"He refused at the last minute," said Lewis. "Had some kind of idea for a new intelligence test. And his partner was too busy putting rats through mazes. Never mind, we don't really need them." Alone of them all, he seemed without worry and foreboding, too busy reaching for the sudden new horizon to consider his own troubles. He wandered over to the buffet and picked up a sandwich and bit into it. "Mmmmm—*delikat*. Sheila, why don't you ditch this long drink of water and marry me?"

"Trade him for a long drink of beer?" she smiled tremulously.

"*Touché!* You've changed too, haven't you? But really, you ought to have done better by me. A long drink of Scotch, at the very least."

"After all," said Corinth gloomily, "it's not as if we were here for any special purpose. I just thought a general discussion would clarify the matter in all our minds and maybe give us some ideas."

Lewis settled himself at the table. "I see the government has finally admitted something is going on," he said, nod-

30

ding at the newspaper which lay beside him. "They had to do it, I suppose, but the admission won't help the panics any. People are afraid, they don't know what to expect, and—well, coming over here, I saw a man run screaming down the street yelling that the end of the world had come. There was a monster-sized revival in Central Park. Three drunks were brawling outside a bar, and not a cop in sight to stop them. I heard fire sirens—big blaze somewhere out Queens way."

Helga lit a cigarette, sucking in her cheeks and half closing her eyes. "John Rossman's in Washington now," she said. After a moment she added to the Mandelbaums: "He came to the Institute a few days back, asked our bright boys to investigate this business but keep their findings confidential, and flew to the capital. With his pull, he'll get the whole story for us if anyone can."

"I don't think there is much of a story yet, to tell the truth," said Mandelbaum. "Just little things like we've all been experiencing, all over the world. They add up to a big upheaval, yes, but there's no over-all picture."

"Just you wait," said Lewis cheerfully. He took another sandwich and a cup of coffee. "I predict that within about one week, things are going to start going to hell in a hand-basket."

"The fact is——" Corinth got out of the chair into which he had flopped and began pacing the room. "The fact is, that the change isn't over. It's still going on. As far as our best instruments can tell—though they're not too exact, what with our instruments being affected themselves—the change is even accelerating."

"Within the limits of error, I think I see a more or less hyperbolic advance," said Lewis. "We've just begun, breth-ren. The way we're going, we'll all have I.Q.'s in the neigh-borhood of 400 within another week."

They sat for a long while, not speaking. Corinth stood with his fists clenched, hanging loose at his sides, and Sheila gave a little wordless cry and ran over to him and hung on his arm. Mandelbaum blew clouds of smoke, scowling as he digested the information; one hand stole out to caress Sarah's, and she squeezed it gratefully. Lewis grinned around his sandwich and went on eating. Helga

31

sat without motion, the long clean curves of her face gone utterly expressionless. The city banged faintly below them, around them.

"What's going to happen?" breathed Sheila at last. She trembled so they could see it. "What's going to happen to us?"

"Christ alone knows," said Lewis, not without gentleness.

"Will it go on building up forever?" asked Sarah.

"Nope," said Lewis. "Can't. It's a matter of neurone chains increasing their speed of reaction, and the intensity of the signals they carry. The physical structure of the cell can take only so much. If they're stimulated too far—insanity, followed by idiocy, followed by death."

"How high can we go?" asked Mandelbaum practically.

"Can't say. The mechanism of the change—and of the nerve cell itself—just isn't known well enough. Anyway, the I.Q. concept is only valid within a limited range; to speak of an I.Q. of 400 really doesn't make sense, intelligence on that level may not be intelligence at all as we know it now, but something else."

Corinth had been too busy with his own work of physical measurements to realize how much Lewis' department knew and theorized. The appalling knowledge was only beginning to grow in him.

"Forget the final results," said Helga sharply. "There's nothing we can do about that. What's important right now is: how do we keep organized civilization going? How do we eat?"

Corinth nodded, mastering the surge of his panic. "Sheer social inertia has carried us along so far," he agreed. "Most people continue in their daily rounds because there's nothing else available. But when things really start changing——"

"The janitor and the elevator man at the Institute quit yesterday," said Helga. "Said the work was too monotonous. What happens when all the janitors and garbage men and ditchdiggers and assembly-line workers decide to quit?"

"They won't all do it," said Mandelbaum. He knocked out his pipe and went over to get some coffee. "Some will

32

be afraid, some will have the sense to see we've got to keep going, some—well, there's no simple answer to this. I agree we're in for a rough period of transition at the very least—people throwing up their jobs, people getting scared, people going crazy in one way or another. What we need is a local interim organization to see us through the next few months. I think the labor unions could be a nucleus— I'm working on that, and when I've got the boys talked and bullied into line, I'm going to approach City Hall with an offer to help."

After a silence, Helga glanced over at Lewis. "You still haven't any idea as to the cause of it all?"

"Oh, yes," said the biologist. "Any number of ideas, and no way of choosing between them. We'll just have to study and think some more, that's all."

"It's a physical phenomenon embracing at least the whole Solar System," declared Corinth. "The observatories have established that much through spectroscopic studies. It may be that the sun, in its orbit around the center of the galaxy, has entered some kind of force-field. But on theoretical grounds—dammit, I won't scrap general relativity till I have to!—on theoretical grounds, I'm inclined to think it's more likely a matter of our having *left* a force-field which slows down light and otherwise affects electromagnetic and electrochemical processes."

"In other words," said Mandelbaum slowly, "we're actually entering a normal state of affairs? All our past has been spent under abnormal conditions?"

"Maybe. Only, of course, those conditions are normal for us. We've evolved under them. We may be like deep-sea fish, which explode when they're brought up to ordinary pressures."

"Heh! Pleasant thought!"

"I don't think I'm afraid to die," said Sheila in a small voice, "but being changed like this——"

"Keep a tight rein on yourself," said Lewis sharply. "I suspect this unbalance is going to drive a lot of people actually insane. Don't be one of them."

He knocked the ash off his cigar. "We have found out some things at the lab," he went on in a dispassionate tone. "As Pete says, it's a physical thing, either a force-field or the lack of one, affecting electronic interactions. The effect is actually rather small, quantitatively. Ordinary chemical reactions go on pretty much as before, in fact I don't think any significant change in the speed of inorganic reactions has been detected. But the more complex and delicate a structure is, the more it feels that slight effect.

"You must have noticed that you're more energetic lately. We've tested basal metabolism rates, and they have increased, not much but some. Your motor reactions are faster too, though you may not have noticed that because your subjective time sense is also speeded up. In other words, not much change in muscular, glandular, vascular, and the other purely somatic functions, just enough to make you feel nervous; and you'll adjust to that pretty quick, if nothing else happens.

"On the other hand, the most highly organized cells— neurones, and above all the neurones of the cerebral cortex—are very much affected. Perception speeds are way up; they measured that over in psych. You've noticed, I'm sure, how much faster you read. Reaction time to all stimuli is less."

"I heard that from Jones," nodded Helga coolly, "and checked up on traffic accident statistics for the past week. Definitely lower. If people react faster, naturally they're better drivers."

"Uh-huh," said Lewis. "Till they start getting tired of poking along at sixty miles an hour and drive at a hundred. Then you may not have any more crack-ups, but those you do have—wham!"

"But if people are smarter," began Sheila, "they'll know enough to——"

"Sorry, no." Mandelbaum shook his head. "Basic personality does not change, right? And intelligent people have always done some pretty stupid or evil things from time to time, just like everybody else. A man might be a brilliant scientist, let's say, but that doesn't stop him from neglecting his health or from driving recklessly or patronizing spiritualists or——"

"Or voting Democrat," nodded Lewis, grinning. "That's correct, Felix. Eventually, no doubt, increased intelligence would affect the total personality, but right now you're not

34

removing anyone's weaknesses, ignorances, prejudices, blind spots, or ambitions; you're just giving him more power, of energy and intelligence, to indulge them—which is one reason why civilization is cracking up."

His voice became dry and didactic: "Getting back to where we were, the most highly organized tissue in the world is, of course, the human cerebrum, the gray matter or seat of consciousness if you like. It feels the stimulus— or lack of inhibition, if Pete's theory is right—more than anything else on Earth. Its functioning increases out of all proportion to the rest of the organism. Maybe you don't know how complex a structure the human brain is. Believe me, it makes the sidereal universe look like a child's building set. There are many times more possible interneuronic connections than there are atoms in the entire cosmos—the factor is something like ten to the power of several million. It's not surprising that a slight change in electrochemistry—too slight to make any important difference to the body—will change the whole nature of the mind. Look what a little dope or alcohol will do, and then remember that this new factor works on the very basis of the cell's existence. The really interesting question is whether so finely balanced a function can survive such a change at all."

There was no fear in his tones, and the eyes behind their heavy lenses held a flash of impersonal excitement. To him this was sheer wonder; Corinth imagined him dying and taking clinical notes on himself as life faded.

"Well," said the physicist grayly, "we'll know pretty soon."

"How can you just sit there and talk about it that way?" cried Sheila. Horror shook her voice.

"My dear girl," said Helga, "do you imagine we can, at this stage, do anything else?"

CHAPTER 5

Selections from *The New York Times*, June 30:

CHANGE DECELERATING

Decline Noted, Effects
Apparently Irreversible

Rhayader Theory May
Hold Explanation

UNIFIED FIELD THEORY ANNOUNCED

Rhayader Announces Extension of Einstein
Theories—Interstellar Travel
a Theoretical Possibility

FEDERAL GOVERNMENT MAY RESIGN FUNCTIONS

President Asks Local Authorities
to Exercise Discretion

N. Y. Labor Authority Under Mandelbaum
Pledges Co-operation

REVOLUTION REPORTED IN
SOVIETIZED COUNTRIES

News Blackout Declared—Organized
Insurrection Spreading

Revolutionaries May Have Developed New
Weapons and Military Concepts

WORLD ECONOMIC CRISIS WORSENING

Food Riots in Paris, Dublin,
Rome, Hong Kong

Shipping Approaches Complete Stand-
still as Thousands of Workers Quit

THIRD BA'AL CULT REVOLTS IN LOS ANGELES

**National Guard Demoralized
Fanatics Seize Key Points—
Street Fighting Continues**

**N. Y. City Hall Warns of Local
Activities of Cultists**

TIGER KILLS ATTENDANT, ESCAPES FROM BRONX ZOO

Police Issue Warning, Organize Hunt

Authorities Consider Shooting All Formidable Specimens

FRESH RIOTING FEARED IN HARLEM

**Police Chief: 'Yesterday's Affair
Only a Beginning'—Mounting Panic
Seems Impossible to Halt**

PSYCHIATRIST SAYS MAN CHANGED 'BEYOND COMPREHENSION'

**Kearnes of Bellevue: 'Unpredictable Results
of Neural Speed-up Make Old Data and Methods
of Control Invalid—Impossible Even to
Guess Ultimate Outcome'**

They had no issue the following day; there was no newsprint to be had.

Brock thought it was strange to be left in charge of the estate. But a lot of funny things had been happening lately.

First Mr. Rossman had gone. Then, the very next day, Stan Wilmer had been attacked by the pigs when he went in to feed them. They charged him, grunting and squealing, stamping him down under their heavy bodies, and several had to be shot before they left him. Most had rushed the fence then, hitting it together and breaking through and disappearing into the woods. Wilmer was pretty badly hurt and had to be taken to the hospital; he swore he'd never come back. Two of the hands had quit the same day.

Brock was in too much of a daze, too full of the change within himself, to care. He didn't have much to do, anyway, now that all work except the most essential was suspended. He looked after the animals, careful to treat them well and to wear a gun at his hip, and had little trouble. Joe was always beside him. The rest of the time he sat around reading, or just with his chin in his hand to think.

Bill Bergen called him in a couple of days after the pig episode. The overseer didn't seem to have changed much, not outwardly. He was still tall and sandy and slow-spoken, with the same toothpick worried between his lips, the same squinted pale eyes. But he spoke even more slowly and cautiously than he had done before to Brock—or did it only seem that way?

"Well, Archie," he said, "Smith just quit."

Brock shifted from one foot to another, looking at the floor.

"Said he wanted to go to college. I couldn't talk him out of it." Bergen's voice held a faintly amused contempt. "The idiot. There won't be any more colleges in another month. That leaves just you and my wife and Voss and me."

"Kind of short-handed," mumbled Brock, feeling he ought to say something.

"One man can do the bare essentials if he must," said Bergen. "Lucky it's summer. The horses and cows can stay out of doors, which saves barn cleaning."

"How about the crops?"

"Not much to do there yet. To hell with them, anyway."

Brock stared upward. In all his years on the place, Bergen had been the steadiest and hardest worker they had.

"You've gotten smart like the rest of us, haven't you, Archie?" asked Bergen. "I daresay you're about up to normal now—pre-change normal, I mean. And it isn't over. You'll get brighter yet."

Brock's face grew hot.

"Sorry, I didn't mean anything personal. You're a good man." He sat for a moment fiddling with the papers on his desk. Then: "Archie, you're in charge here now."

"Huh?"

"I'm leaving too."

"But, Bill—you can't——"

"Can and will, Archie." Bergen stood up. "You know, my wife always wanted to travel, and I have some things to think out. Never mind what they are, it's something I've puzzled over for many years and now I believe I see an answer. We're taking our car and heading west."

"But—but—Mr. Rossman—he's de-pen-ding on you, Bill——"

"I'm afraid that there are more important things in life than Mr. Rossman's country retreat," said Bergen evenly. "You can handle the place all right, even if Voss leaves too."

Fright and bewilderment lashed into scorn: "Scared of the animals, huh?"

"Why, no, Archie. Always remember that you're still brighter than they are, and what's more important, you have hands. A gun will stop anything." Bergen walked over to the window and looked out. It was a bright windy day with sunlight torn in the restless branches of trees. "As a matter of fact," he went on in the same gentle, remote tone, "a farm is safer than any other place I can think of. If the production and distribution systems break down, as they may, you'll still have something to eat. But my wife and I aren't getting any younger. I've been a steady, sober, conscientious man all my life. Now I wonder what all the fuss and the lost years were about."

He turned his back. "Good-by, Archie." It was a command.

Brock went out into the yard, shaking his head and muttering to himself. Joe whined uneasily and nuzzled his palm. He ruffled the golden fur and sat down on a bench and put his head in his hands.

The trouble is, he thought, *that while the animals and I got smarter, so did everybody else. God in Heaven—what sort of things are going on inside Bill Bergen's skull?*

It was a terrifying concept. The speed and scope and sharpness of his own mind were suddenly cruel. He dared not think what a normal human might be like by now.

Only it was hard to realize. Bergen hadn't become a god. His eyes didn't blaze, his voice was not vibrant and resolute, he didn't start building great engines that flamed and roared. He was still a tall stoop-shouldered man with a weary face, a patient drawl, nothing else. The trees were still green, a bird chattered behind a rosebush, a fly rested cobalt-blue on the arm of the bench.

Brock remembered, vaguely, sermons from the few times he had been in church. The end of the world—was the sky going to open up, would the angels pour down the vials of wrath on a shaking land, and would God appear to judge the sons of man? He listened for the noise of great galloping hoofs, but there was only the wind in the trees.

That was the worst of it. The sky didn't care. The Earth went on turning through an endlessness of dark and silence, and what happened in the thin scum seething over its crust didn't matter.

Nobody cared. It wasn't important.

Brock looked at his scuffed shoes and then at the strong hairy hands between his knees. They seemed impossibly alien, the hands of a stranger. *Sweet Jesus,* he thought, *is this really happening to me?*

He grabbed Joe by the ruffed neck and held him close. Suddenly he had a wild need for a woman, someone to hold him and talk to him and block out the loneliness of the sky.

He got up, sweat cold on his body, and walked over to the Bergens' cottage. It was his now, he supposed.

Voss was a young fellow, a kid from town who wasn't very bright and hadn't been able to find any other employment. He looked moodily up from a book as the other man entered the small living room.

"Well," said Brock, "Bill just quit."

"I know. What're we gonna do?" Voss was scared and weak and willing to surrender leadership. Bergen must have foreseen that. The sense of responsibility was strengthening.

"We'll be all right if we stay here," said Brock. "Just wait it out, keep going, that's all."

"The animals——"

"You got a gun, don't you? Anyway, they'll know when they're well off. Just be careful, always lock the gates behind you, treat 'em good——"

"I'm not gonna wait on any damn animals," said Voss sullenly.

"That you are, though." Brock went over to the icebox and took out two cans of beer and opened them.

"Look here, I'm smarter than you are, and——"

"And I'm stronger'n you. If you don't like it, you can

40

quit. I'm staying." Brock gave Voss one can and tilted the other to his mouth.

"Look," he said after a moment, "I know those animals. They're mostly habit. They'll stick around because they don't know any better and because we feed 'em and because—uh—respect for man has been drilled into 'em. There ain't no bears or wolves in the woods, nothing that can give us trouble except maybe the pigs. Me, I'd be more scared to be in a city."

"How come?" Despite himself, Voss was overmastered. He laid down the book and took up his beer. Brock glanced at the title: *Night of Passion,* in a two-bit edition. Voss might have gained a better mind, but that didn't change him otherwise. He just didn't want to think.

"The people," said Brock. "Christ knows what they'll do." He went over to the radio and turned it on and presently got a newscast. It didn't mean much to him; mostly it was about the new brain power, but the words were strung together in a way that didn't make a lot of sense. The voice sounded frightened, though.

After lunch, Brock decided to take a scout through the woods and see if he couldn't locate the pigs and find out what they were up to. They worried him more than he would admit. Pigs had always been smarter than most people knew. They might also get to thinking about the stores of feed kept on a farm watched by only two men.

Voss wasn't even asked to come; he'd have refused, and in any event it was wise to keep one man on guard at home. Brock and Joe went over the fence and into the six hundred acres of forest alone.

It was green and shadowy and full of rustling in there. Brock went quietly, a rifle under one arm, parting the underbrush before him with habitual ease. He saw no squirrels, though they were ordinarily plentiful. Well—they must have thought it out, the way crows had done long ago, and seen that a man with a gun was something to stay away from. He wondered how many eyes were watching him, and what was going on behind the eyes. Joe stuck close to his heels, not bounding on all sides as he normally did.

An overlooked branch slapped viciously at the man's

face. He stood for an instant of creeping fear. Were the trees thinking too, now? Was the whole world going to rise in revolt?

No— After a moment he got control of himself and went stolidly on along the sheep trail. To be changed by this—whatever-it-was—a thing had to be able to think in the first place. Trees had no brains. He seemed to recall hearing once that insects didn't either, and made a note to check up on this. Good thing that Mr. Rossman had a big library.

And a good thing, Brock realized, that he himself was steady. He had never gotten too excited about anything, and was taking the new order more calmly than seemed possible. One step at a time, that was it. Just go along from day to day, doing as much as he could to stay alive.

The thicket parted before him and a pig looked out. It was an old black boar, a big mean-looking creature which stood immovably in his path. The snouted face was a mask, but Brock had never seen anything so cold as its eyes. Joe bristled, growling, and Brock lifted the rifle. They stood that way for a long time, not moving. Then the boar grunted—it seemed contemptuous—and turned and slipped into the shadows. Brock realized that his body was wet.

He forced himself to go on for a couple of hours, ranging the woods but seeing little. When he came back, he was sunk in thought. The animals had changed, all right, but he had no way of telling how much, or what they would do next. Maybe nothing.

"I been thinking," said Voss when he entered the cottage. "Maybe we should move in with another farmer. Ralph Martinson needs extra help, now his hired man has quit."

"I'm staying."

Voss gave him a cool glance. "Because you don't want to go back to being a moron, huh?"

Brock winced, but made his answer flat. "Call it what you like."

"I'm not going to stay here forever."

"Nobody asked you to. Come on, it's about time for the milking."

"Judas, what'll we do with the milk from thirty cows?

The creamery truck ain't come around for three days."

"Mmmmm—yeah— Well, I'll figger out something. Right now, we can't let 'em bust their teats."

"Can't we just?" muttered Voss, but followed him out to the barn.

Milking thirty cows was a big job, even with a couple of machines to help. Brock decided to dry up most of them, but that would take some time, you had to taper them off gradually. Meanwhile they were restless and hard to control.

He came out and took a pitchfork and began throwing hay over the fence to the sheep, which had flocked in from the woods as usual. Halfway through the job, he was roused by Joe's wild yammer. He turned and saw the farm's enormous Holstein bull approaching.

He's loose! Brock's hand went to the pistol at his belt, then back to his fork. A popgun wasn't much use against such a monster. The bull snorted, pawing the ground and shaking his horn-cropped head.

"Okay, fella." Brock went slowly toward him, wiping sandy lips with his tongue. The noise of his heart was loud in his ears. "Okay, easy, back to the pen with yuh."

Joe snarled, stiff-legged beside his master. The bull lowered his head and charged.

Brock braced himself. The giant before him seemed to fill the sky.

Brock stabbed under the jaw. It was a mistake, he realized wildly, he should have gone for the eyes. The fork ripped out of his hands and he felt a blow which knocked him to the ground. The bull ground his head against Brock's chest, trying to gore with horns that weren't there.

Suddenly he bellowed, a horror of pain in his voice. Joe had come behind him and fastened jaws in the right place. The bull turned, one hoof grating along Brock's ribs. The man got his gun out and fired from the ground. The bull began to run. Brock rolled over, scrambled to his feet, and sprang alongside the great head. He put the pistol behind one ear and fired. The bull stumbled, falling to his knees. Brock emptied the gun into his skull.

After that he collapsed on the body, whirling toward darkness.

43

He came to as Voss shook him.

"Are yuh hurt, Archie?" The words gibbered meaninglessly in his ears. "Are you hurt?"

Brock let Voss lead him into the cottage. After a stiff drink he felt better and inspected himself. "I'm all right," he muttered. "Bruises and cuts, no bones broke. I'm okay."

"That settles it." Voss was shaking worse than Brock. "We're leaving here."

The red head shook. "No."

"Are you crazy? Alone here, all the animals running wild, everything gone to hell—are you crazy?"

"I'm staying."

"I'm not! I got half a mind to make you come along."

Joe growled. "Don't," said Brock. He felt, suddenly, nothing but an immense weariness. "You go if you want to, but leave me. I'll be all right."

"Well——"

"I'll herd some of the stock over to Martinson's tomorrow, if he'll take 'em. I can handle the rest myself."

Voss argued for a while longer, then gave up and took the jeep and drove away. Brock smiled without quite knowing why he did.

He checked the bull's pen. The gate had been broken down by a determined push. Half the power of fences had always lain in the fact that animals didn't know enough to keep shoving at them. Well, now they did, it seemed.

"I'll have to bury that fellow with a bulldozer," said Brock. It was becoming more and more natural for him to speak aloud to Joe. "Do it tomorrow. Let's have supper, boy, and then we'll read and play some music. We're alone from here on, I guess."

CHAPTER 6

A CITY was an organism, but Corinth had never appreciated its intricate and precarious equilibrium before. Now, with the balance gone, New York was sliding swiftly toward disruption and death.

Only a few subways were running, an emergency system manned by those devoted enough to stay by a job which had become altogether flat and distasteful. The stations were hollow and dark, filthy with unswept litter, and the shrieking of wheels held a tormented loneliness. Corinth walked to work, along dirty streets whose traffic had fallen to a reckless fragment of the old steady river.

Memory, five days old: *the roads jammed, a steel barricade ten miles long, honking and yelling till the high windows shivered, filling the air with exhaust fumes till men choked—blind panic, a mob fleeing a city they had decided was finished, flying from it at an estimated average speed of five miles an hour. Two cars had locked bumpers and the drivers got out and fought till their faces were bloody masks. Police helicopters had buzzed impotently overhead, like monster flies. It was saddening to know that multiplied intelligence had not quenched such an animal stampede.*

Those who remained—probably three-fourths of the city's dwellers—were still scraping along. Severely rationed gas, water, and electricity were being supplied. Food still trickled in from the country, though you had to take what you could get and pay exorbitantly. But it was like a pot, rumbling and seething and gathering itself to boil over.

Memory, three days old: *the second Harlem riot, when fear of the unknown and rage at ancient injustice had stood up to fight, for no reason except that untrained minds could not control their own new powers. The huge roar of burn-*

45

ing tenements, giant red flames flapping against a windy
night sky. The restless luminance like blood on a thousand
dark faces, a thousand ill-clad bodies that stamped and
swayed and struggled in the streets. A knife gleaming high
and slaking itself in a human throat. A broken howling
under the noise of fire. A scream as some woman went
down and was stamped shapeless beneath a hundred run-
ning feet. The helicopters tossing and twisting in the storm
of superheated air rushing up from the flames. And in the
morning, empty streets, a haze of bitter smoke, a dim
sobbing behind shuttered windows.

Yes, still a thin tight-held semblance of order. Only—
how long could it endure?

A tattered man with a ragged, new-looking beard was
ranting on a street corner. Some dozen people stood around
him, listening with a strange intensity. Corinth heard the
words loud and harsh in the quiet: "—because we forgot
the eternal principles of life, because we let the scientists
betray us, because we all followed the eggheads. I tell you,
it is life only that matters before the great Oneness in
whom all are one and one are all. Behold, I bring you the
word of the returned——"

His skin crawled, and he made a swift detour around
that corner. Was it a missionary of the Third Ba'al cultists?
He didn't know, and didn't feel like stopping to find out.
Not a cop in sight to report it to. There was going to be
real trouble if the new religion got many followers here in
town. It gave him some comfort to see a woman entering
the Catholic church nearby.

A taxi rounded a corner on two wheels, sideswiped a
parked car, and was gone in a burst of noise. Another
automobile crept slowly down the street, the driver tight-
faced, his passenger holding a shotgun. Fear. The shops
were boarded up on either side; one small grocery remained open, and its proprietor carried a pistol at his belt.
In the dingy entrance to an apartment house, an old man
sat reading Kant's *Critique* with a strange and frantic
hunger which ignored the world around him.

"Mister, I haven't eaten for two days."

Corinth looked at the shape which had slunk out of an
alley. "Sorry," he answered. "I've only got ten bucks on

me. Barely enough for a meal at present prices."

"Christ, I can't find work——"

"Go to City Hall, friend. They'll give you a job and see that you're fed. They need men badly."

Scorn: "That outfit? Sweeping streets, hauling garbage, trucking in food—I'd starve first!"

"Starve, then," spat Corinth, and went on more swiftly. The weight of the revolver dragging down his coat pocket was cheering. He had little sympathy for that type, after what he had seen.

Though could you expect anything different? You take a typical human, a worker in factory or office, his mind dulled to a collection of verbal reflexes, his future a day-to-day plodding which offered him no more than a chance to fill his belly and be anesthesized by a movie or his television —more and bigger automobiles, more and brighter plastics, onward and upward with the American Way of Life. Even before the change, there had been an inward hollowness in Western civilization, an unconscious realization that there ought to be more in life than one's own ephemeral self—and the ideal had not been forthcoming.

Then suddenly, almost overnight, human intelligence had exploded toward fantastic heights. An entire new cosmos opened before this man, visions, realizations, thought boiling unbidden within him. He saw the miserable inadequacy of his life, the triviality of his work, the narrow and meaningless limits of his beliefs and conventions—and he resigned.

Not everyone left, of course—not even the majority. But enough people did to throw the whole structure of technological civilization out of gear. If no more coal was being mined, then the makers of steel and of machines could not stay by their jobs even if they wanted to. Add to that the disturbances caused by emotions gone awry, and——

A naked woman walked down the street, carrying a market basket. She had set out to think for herself, Corinth imagined, and had decided that clothes in summer were ridiculous, and had taken advantage of the fact that the police had other worries to shed hers. No harm in that per se, but as a symptom it made him shiver. Any society

47

was necessarily founded on certain more or less arbitrary rules and restrictions. Too many people had suddenly realized that the laws were arbitrary, without intrinsic significance, and had proceeded to violate whichever ones they didn't like.

A young man sat on a doorstep, his arms clasped about knees drawn up under his chin, rocking to and fro and whimpering softly. Corinth stopped. "What's wrong?" he asked.

"Fear." The eyes were bright and glazed. "I suddenly realized it. I am alone."

Corinth's mind leaped ahead to what he was going to say, but he heard out the panic-blurred words: "All I know, all I am, is here, in my head. Everything exists for me only as I know it. And someday I'm going to die." A line of spittle ran from one corner of his mouth. "Someday the great darkness will come, I will not be—nothing will be! You may still exist, for you—though how can I tell that you aren't just a dream of mine?—but for me there will be nothing, nothing, nothing. I will never even have been." The weak tears dribbled out of his eyes, and Corinth went on.

Insanity—yes, that had a lot to do with the collapse. There must be millions who had not been able to stand that sudden range and sharpness of comprehension. They hadn't been able to handle their new power, and it had driven them mad.

He shuddered in the hot still air.

The Institute was like a haven. When he walked in, a man sat on guard: submachine gun lying beside his chair, chemistry text on his lap. The face that lifted to Corinth's was serene. "Hullo."

"Had any trouble, Jim?"

"Not yet. But you never can tell, with all the prowlers and fanatics."

Corinth nodded, feeling some of the clamminess leave him. There were still rational men who did not go kiting off after suddenly perceived stars, but stuck quietly to the immediate work.

The elevator attendant was a seven-year-old boy, son of a man in the Institute; schools were closed. "Hi, sir," he said cheerily. "I been waiting for you. How on earth did Maxwell work out his equations?"

"Huh?" Corinth's eyes fell on a book lying on the seat. "Oh, you've been studying radio, have you? Cadogan is pretty stiff to start out on, you should try reading——"

"I seen circuit diagrams, Mr. Corinth. I wanna know why they work, only Cadogan here just gives the equations."

Corinth referred him to a text on vector calculus. "When you've been through that, come see me again." He was smiling when he got off on the seventh floor, but his smile faded as he walked down the corridor.

Lewis was in his laboratory, waiting for him. "Late," he grunted.

"Sheila," replied Corinth.

The conversation here was rapidly becoming a new language. When your mind was of quadrupled capability, a single word, a gesture of hand, a flicker of expression, could convey more to one who knew you and your mannerisms than whole paragraphs of grammatical English.

"You're late this morning," Lewis had meant. "Have any trouble?"

"I got started late because of Sheila," Corinth had told him. "She's not taking this well at all, Nat, frankly, I'm worried about her. Only what can I do? I don't understand human psychology any more, it's changing too much and too fast. Nobody does. We're all becoming strangers to each other—to ourselves—and it's frightening."

Lewis's heavy body moved forward. "Come on. Rossman's here and wants a confab with us."

They went down the corridor, leaving Johansson and Grunewald immersed in their work: measuring the changed constants of nature, recalibrating instruments, performing all the enormous basic labor of science again from the ground up.

Throughout the building the other departments mapped out the altered faces of their own disciplines. Cybernetics, chemistry, biology, above all psychology—men grudged the time for sleep, there was so much to do.

The department heads were gathered around a long table in the main conference room. Rossman sat at its end, tall and thin and white-haired, no movement in his austere features. Helga Arnulfsen was at his right and Felix Mandelbaum at his left. For an instant Corinth wondered what the labor organizer was doing here, then realized that he must be representing the emergency city government.

"Good day, gentlemen." Rossman went through the forms of Edwardian courtesy with a punctilio that would have been laughable if it were not so obviously a desperate effort to cling to something real and known. "Please be seated."

Everyone seemed to be here now, for Rossman got directly to business:

"I have just returned from Washington. I have called you together because I feel that an exchange of ideas and information is urgently needed. You will feel better for knowing what I can give you of the over-all picture, and I will certainly be happier for what scientific explanation you have found. Together we may be able to plan intelligently."

"As for the explanation," said Lewis, "we've pretty well agreed here at the Institute that Dr. Corinth's theory is the right one. This postulates a force-field of partly electromagnetic character, generated by gyromagnetic action within atomic nuclei near the center of the galaxy. It radiates outward in a cone which, by the time it has reached our section of space, is many light-years across. Its effect has been to inhibit certain electromagnetic and electrochemical processes, among which the functioning of certain types of neurones is prominent. We suppose that the Solar System, in its orbit around galactic center, entered this force-field many millions of years ago—hardly later than the Cretaceous. Doubtless many species of that time died out. However, life as a whole survived—adapted nervous systems compensated for the inhibiting force by becoming that much more efficient. In short, all life forms today are—or were, immediately before the change—about as intelligent as they would have been anyway."

"I see," nodded Rossman. "And then the sun and its planets moved out of the force-field."

"Yes. The field must have a rather sharp boundary, as

such things go in astronomy, for the change took place within a few days. The fringe of the field—from the region of full intensity to the region of no effect at all—is perhaps only ten million miles wide. We're definitely out of it now; physical constants have remained stable for several days."

"But our minds haven't," said Mandelbaum bleakly.

"I know," cut in Lewis. "We'll come to that in a minute. The general effect of Earth's coming out of the inhibitor field was, of course, a sudden zooming of intelligence in every life form possessing a brain. Suddenly the damping force to which every living organism was adjusted, was gone.

"Naturally, the lack of that force has produced an enormous unbalance. Nervous systems have tended to run wild, trying to stabilize and function on a new level; that's why everybody felt so jumpy and frightened to begin with. The physical layout of the brain is adapted to one speed—one set of speeds, rather—of neurone signals; now suddenly the speed is increased while the physical structure remains the same. In plain language, it'll take us a while to get used to this."

"Why aren't we dead?" asked Grahovitch, the chemist. "I should think our hearts and so on would start working like mad."

"The autonomic nervous system has been relatively little affected," said Lewis. "It seems to be a matter of cellular type; there are many different kinds of nerve cells, you know, and apparently only those in the cerebral cortex have reacted much to the change. Even there, the rate of functioning has not really gone up much—the factor is small—but apparently the processes involved in consciousness are so sensitive that it has made an enormous difference to what we call thought."

"But we will survive?"

"Oh, yes, I'm sure no physiological damage will result —to most people, anyway. Some have gone insane, to be sure, but that's probably more for psychological than histological reasons."

"And—will we enter another such force-field?" queried Rossman.

"Hardly," said Corinth. "On the basis of theory, I'm pretty sure there can only be one such, at most, in any galaxy. With the sun requiring some two hundred million years for its orbit around galactic center—well, we should have more than half that period before we have to start worrying about getting stupid again."

"M-hm. I see, gentlemen. Thank you very much." Rossman leaned forward, clasping his thin fingers before him. "Now as to what I have been able to find out, I fear it is not much, and that little is bad news. Washington is a madhouse. Many key men have already left their posts; it seems that there are more important things in life than administering Public Law Number Such and such——"

"Well, I'm afraid they're right," grinned Lewis sardonically.

"No doubt. But let us face it, gentlemen; however little we may like the present system we cannot scrap it overnight."

"What's the word from overseas?" asked Weller, the mathematician. "How about Russia?"

"We'd be helpless against an armed attack," said Rossman, "but what military intelligence we have left indicates that the Soviet dictatorship is having troubles of its own." He sighed. "First things first, gentlemen. We have to worry about our own breakdown. Washington grows more helpless every day: fewer and fewer people listen to the President's commands and appeals, less and less force is at his disposal. In many areas martial law has already been declared, but any attempt to enforce it would only mean civil war. Reorganization is going to have to be on a local basis. That is essentially the news I bring to you."

"We've been working on it, here in New York," said Mandelbaum. He looked tired, burned out by days and nights of unresting effort. "I've got the unions pretty well into line by now. Arrangement. will be made to bring in and distribute food, and we hope to get a volunteer militia to maintain some kind of order."

He turned to Rossman. "You're an able organizer. Your other interests, your businesses and your factories, are going down the drain, and here's a job which has to be done. Will you help us?"

"Of course," nodded the old man. "And the Institute——"

"Will have to keep going. We've got to understand just what's happened and what we can expect in the near future. We've got to have a thousand things developed immediately if not sooner."

The talk turned to organizational details. Corinth had little to say. He was too worried about Sheila. Last night she had woken up screaming.

CHAPTER 7

WATO the witch doctor was tracing figures in the dust outside his thatch hut and muttering to himself. M'Wanzi heard him through the clank of weapons and the thick voices of the drums, as tall warriors passed back and forth: "——the law of similarity, that like causes like, may be expressed in the form *ya* or not-*ya*, thus showing that this form of magic obeys the rule of universal causality. But how to fit in the law of contagion——?"

M'Wanzi threw him an amused look as he strode by. Let the old man build his dusty dreams as he wished. The rifle on his shoulder was solid reality and enough for him. And it would be guns and not magic which fulfilled an ancient wish.

Free the black man! Drive the white oppressors back beyond the sea! Since his youth and the days of horror on the plantation, it had been his life. But only now——

Well, he had not been frightened by that which was happening within his soul, as the others were. He had seized this power to think with a swift fierce gladness, and his will had dominated whole tribes driven half-crazy with fear, ready to turn anywhere for the comfort of leadership. Over thousands of miles, from Congo jungles to the veldts of the south, men tormented and enslaved and spat upon

53

had lifted weary faces to a message blown down the wind. Now was the time to strike, before the white man also rallied—the scheme was ready, lying in the soul of M'Wanzi the Elephant, the campaign was planned in a few flashing days, the subtle tongue won over leaders of a hundred conflicting groups, the army was stirring to life, now was the time to be free!

The drums talked around him as he went toward the edge of the jungle. He stepped through a wall of canebrake into the thick hot shadows of the forest. Another shadow moved down, flitted across the earth and waited grotesquely before him. Wise brown eyes regarded him with an inborn sadness.

"Have you gathered the brethren of the forest?" asked M'Wanzi.

"They come soon," said the ape.

That had been M'Wanzi's great realization. All the rest, the organization, the planned campaign, that was nothing beside this: that if the souls of men had suddenly grown immensely bigger, so also the souls of animals must have grown. His guess had been confirmed by terrified stories of raids on farms made by elephants of demoniac cunning, but when those reports came he was already working out a common language of clicks and grunts with a captured chimpanzee. The apes had never been much less intelligent than man, M'Wanzi suspected. Today he could offer them much in exchange for their help; and were they not Africans too?

"My brother of the forest, go tell your people to make ready."

"Not all of them wish this thing, brother of the fields. They must be beaten before they wish it. That takes time."

"Time we have little of. Use the drums as I taught you. Send word throughout the land and let the hosts gather at the appointed places."

"It shall be as you wish. When next the moon rises full, the children of the forest shall be there, and they shall be armed with knives and blowguns and assagais as you showed me."

"Brother of the forest, you have gladdened my heart. Go with fortune and carry that word."

The ape turned and swung lithely up a tree. A stray sunbeam gleamed off the rifle slung at his back.

Corinth sighed, yawned, and got up from his desk, shoving the papers away. He did not say anything aloud, but to his assistants, hunched over some testing apparatus, the meaning was clear: (To hell with it. I'm too tired to think straight any more. Going home.).

Johansson gestured with his hand, conveying as well as if he had spoken: (Think I'll stay here for a while, chief. This gimmick is shaping up nicely.). Grunewald added a curt nod.

Corinth fumbled automatically for a cigarette, but his pocket was empty. Smokes just weren't to be had these days. He hoped the world would get back on an operating basis soon, but it seemed less likely every day. What was happening outside the city? A few radio stations, professional and amateur, were maintaining a tenuous web of communications across western Europe, the Americas, and the Pacific, but the rest of the planet seemed to be swallowed by darkness—an occasional report of violence, like lightning in the night, and then nothing.

Mandelbaum had warned him yesterday to be on his guard. Missionaries of the Third Ba'al were definitely known to have entered the city despite all precautions and were making converts right and left. The new religion seemed to be wholly orgiastic, with a murderous hatred for logic and science and rationality of all kinds—you could expect trouble.

Corinth went down hallways that were tunnels of dusk. Electricity must be conserved; only a few power stations were still operating, manned and guarded by volunteers. Elevator service ended at sunset, and he walked down seven flights to ground level. Loneliness oppressed him, and when he saw a light in Helga's office he paused, startled, and then knocked.

"Come in."

He opened the door. She sat behind a littered desk, writing up some kind of manifest. The symbols she used were strange to him, probably her own invention and more efficient than the conventional ones. She still looked as severely handsome, but there was a deep weariness that paled her eyes.

"Hullo, Pete," she said. The smile that twitched her mouth was tired, but it had warmth. "How've you been?"

Corinth spoke two words and made three gestures; she filled in his intention from logic and her knowledge of his old speech habits: (Oh—all right. But you—I thought you'd been co-opted by Felix to help whip his new government into shape.).

(I have,) she implied. (But I feel more at home here, and it's just as good a place to do some of my work. Who've you got on my old job, by the way?)

(Billy Saunders—ten years of age, but a sharp kid. Maybe we should get a moron, though. The physical strain may be too much for a child.)

(I doubt it. There isn't much to do now, really. You boys co-operate pretty smoothly since the change—unlike the rest of the world!)

"I don't know if it's safe for you to come so far from where you live." Corinth shifted awkwardly on his feet. "Look, let me take you home."

"Not necessary." She spoke with a certain bite in her tones, and Corinth realized dully that she loved him.

And all our feelings have intensified. I never knew before how much of man's emotional life is bound up with his brain, how much more keenly he feels than any other animal.

"Sit down," she invited, leaning back in her seat. "Rest for a minute."

He smiled wearily, lowering himself into a chair. "Wish we had some beer," he murmured. (It'd be like the old days.)

"The old days—the lost innocence. We'll always regret them, won't we? We'll always look back on our blindness with a wistful longing that the new generation simply won't understand." She beat a clenched fist against the desk top, very softly. The light gleamed gold in her hair.

"How's your work coming along?" she asked after a moment. The silence hummed around them.

"Good enough. I've been in touch with Rhayader in England, over the short wave. They're having a tough time,

56

but keeping alive. Some of their biochemists are working on yeasts, getting good results. By the end of the year they hope to be able to feed themselves adequately, if not very palatably as yet—food synthesis plants being built. He gave me some information that just about clinched the theory of the inhibitor field—how it's created. I've got Johansson and Grunewald at work on an apparatus to generate a similar field on a small scale; if they succeed, we'll know that our hypothesis is probably right. Then Nat can use the apparatus to study biological effects in detail. As for me, I'm going into the development of Rhayader's general relativity-cum-quantum mechanics—applying a new variation of communications theory, of all things, to help me out."

"What's your purpose, other than curiosity?"

"Quite practical, I assure you. We may find a way to generate atomic energy from any material whatsoever, by direct nucleonic disintegration: no more fuel problems. We may even find a way to travel faster than light. The stars— well——"

"New worlds. Or we might return to the inhibitor field, out in space—why not? Go back to being stupid. Maybe we'll be happier that way. No, no, I realize you can't go home again." Helga opened a drawer and took out a crumpled packet. "Smoke?"

"Angel! How on earth did you manage that?"

"I have my ways." She struck a match for him and lit her own cigarette with it. "Efficient—yeah."

They smoked in silence for a while, but the knowledge of each other's thoughts was like a pale flickering between them.

"You'd better let me see you home," said Corinth. "It's not safe out there. The prophet's mobs——"

"All right," she said. "Though I've got a car and you haven't."

"It's only a few blocks from your place to mine, in a safe district."

Since it was not possible as yet to patrol the entire sprawling city, the government had concentrated on certain key streets and areas.

Corinth took off his glasses and rubbed his eyes. "I don't

really understand it," he said. "Human relationships were never my long suit, and even now I can't quite—— Well, why should this sudden upsurge of intelligence throw so many back to the animal stage? Why can't they see——?"

"They don't want to." Helga drew hard on her cigarette. "Quite apart from those who've gone insane, and they're an important factor, there remains the necessity of not only having something to think with, but something to think about. You've taken millions—hundreds of millions—of people who've never had an original thought in their lives and suddenly thrown their brains into high gear. They start thinking—but what basis have they got? They still retain the old superstitions, prejudices, hates and fears and greeds, and most of their new mental energy goes to elaborate rationalization of these. Then someone like this Third Ba'al comes along and offers an anodyne to frightened and confused people; he tells them it's all right to throw off this terrible burden of thought and forget themselves in an emotional orgy. It won't last, Pete, but the transition is tough."

"Yeah—hm—I had to get an I.Q. of 500 or so—whatever that means—to appreciate how little brains count for, after all. Nice thought." Corinth grimaced and stubbed out his cigarette.

Helga shuffled her papers together and put them in a drawer. "Shall we go?"

"Might as well. It's close to midnight. Sheila'll be worried, I'm afraid."

They walked out through the deserted lobby, past the guards and into the street. A solitary lamp cast a dull puddle of luminance on Helga's car. She took the wheel and they purred quietly down an avenue of night.

"I wish——" Her voice out of darkness was thin. "I wish I were out of this. Off in the mountains somewhere."

He nodded, suddenly sick with his own need for open sky and the clean light of stars.

The mob was on them so fast that they had no time to escape. One moment they were driving down an empty way between blind walls, the next instant the ground seemed to vomit men. They came pouring from the side streets, quiet save for a murmur of voices and the shuffling of a thousand feet, and the few lamps gleamed off their eyes and teeth. Helga braked to a squealing halt as the surge went in front of them, cutting them off.

"Kill the scientists!" It hung like a riven cloud for a moment, one quavering scream which became a deep chanting. The living stream flowed around the car, veiled in shadow, and Corinth heard their breathing hot and hoarse in his ears.

> Break their bones and burn their homes,
> take their wimmin, the sons of sin,
> wallow hollow an' open the door,
> open an' let the Third Ba'al in!

A sheet of fire ran up behind the tall buildings, something was in flames. The light was like blood on the dripping head which someone lifted on a pole.

They must have broken the line of the patrols, thought Corinth wildly, they must have smashed into this guarded region and meant to lay it waste before reinforcements came.

A face dirty and bearded and stinking shoved in through the driver's window. "Uh woman! He got uh woman here!"

Corinth took the pistol from his coat pocket and fired. Briefly, he was aware of its kick and bark, the stinging of powder grains in his skin. The face hung there for an eternal time, dissolved into blood and smashed bone. Slowly it sagged, and the crowd screamed. The car rocked under their thrusts.

Corinth braced himself, shoving at his own door, jamming it open against the milling press of bodies. Someone clawed at his feet as he scrambled up on the hood. He kicked, feeling his shoe jar against teeth, and stood up. The firelight blazed in his face. He had taken off his glasses, without stopping to think why it was unsafe to be seen wearing them, and the fire and the crowd and the buildings were a shifting blur.

"Now hear me!" he shouted. "Hear me, people of Ba'al!"

A bullet whanged past him, he felt its hornet buzz, but there was no time to be afraid. "Hear the word of the Third Ba'al!"

"Let 'im talk!" It was a bawling somewhere out in that flowing, mumbling, unhuman river of shadows. "Hear his word."

"Lightning and thunder and rain of bombs!" yelled Corinth. "Eat, drink, and be merry, for the end of the world is at hand! Can't you hear the planet cracking under your feet? The scientists have fired the big atomic bomb. We're on our way to kill them before the world breaks open like rotten fruit. Are you with us?"

They halted, muttering, shuffling their feet, uncertain of what they had found. Corinth went on, raving, hardly aware of what he was saying. "—kill and loot and steal the women! Break open the bottle shops! Fire, clean fire, let it burn the scientists who fired the big atomic bomb. This way, brothers! I know where they're hiding. Follow me!"

"Kill them!" The cheering grew, huge and obscene between the cliff walls of Manhattan. The head on the pole bobbed insanely, and firelight wavered off its teeth.

"Down there!" Corinth danced on the hood, gesturing toward Brooklyn. "They're hiding there, people of Ba'al. I saw the big atomic bomb myself, with my own eyes I saw it, and I knew the end of the world was at hand. The Third Ba'al himself sent me to guide you. May his lightnings strike me dead if that ain't the truth!"

Helga blew her horn, an enormous echoing clamor that seemed to drive them into frenzy. Someone began capering, goatlike, and the others joined him, and the mob snake-danced down the street.

Corinth climbed to the ground, shaking uncontrollably. "Follow 'em," he gasped. "They'll get suspicious if we don't follow 'em."

"Sure thing, Pete." Helga helped him inside and trailed the throng. Her headlights glared off their backs. Now and then she blew the horn to urge them on.

There was a whirring high in heaven. Corinth's breath whistled between his teeth. "Let's go," he mumbled.

Helga nodded, made a U-turn, and shot back down the avenue. Behind them, the mob scattered as police helicopters sprayed them with tear gas.

After a silent while, Helga halted before Corinth's place. "Here we are," she said.

"But I was going to see you home," he said feebly.

"You did. Also you stopped those creatures from doing a lot of harm, to the district as well as us." The vague light glimmered off her smile, it was shaky and tears lay in her eyes. "That was wonderful, Pete. I didn't know you could do it."

"Neither did I," he said huskily.

"Maybe you missed your calling. More money in revivals, I'm told. Well—" She sat for a moment, then: "Well, good night."

"Good night," he said.

She leaned forward, lips parted as if she were about to say something more. Then she clamped them shut, shook her head. The slamming of the door was loud and empty as she drove off.

Corinth stood looking after the car till it was out of sight. Then he turned slowly and entered his building.

CHAPTER 8

SUPPLIES were running low—food for himself, feed and salt for the animals left to him. There was no electricity, and he didn't like to use fuel in the gasoline lamp he had found. Brock decided that he would have to go to town.

"Stay here, Joe," he said. "I ought to be back soon."

The dog nodded, an uncannily human gesture. He was picking up English fast; Brock had a habit of talking to him and had lately begun a deliberate program of education. "Keep an eye on things, Joe," he said, looking uneasily to the edge of the woods.

He filled the tank of a battered green pickup from the estate's big drums, got in, and went down the driveway. It was a cool, hazy morning, the smell of rain was in the air and the horizon lay blurred. As he rattled down the county road, he thought that the countryside was utterly deserted.

What was it—two months—since the change? Maybe there wouldn't be anyone in town at all.

Turning off on the paved state highway, he pushed the accelerator till the motor roared. He wasn't eager to visit normal humanity, and wanted to get it over with. His time alone had been peaceful—plenty of hard work, yes, to keep him busy; but when he wasn't too occupied or tired he was reading and thinking, exploring the possibilities of a mind which by now, he supposed, was that of a high-order genius by pre-change standards. He had settled down phlegmatically to an anchorite's life—there were worse fates—and didn't relish meeting the world again.

He had gone over to Martinson's, the neighbor's, a few days ago, but no one had been there, the place was boarded up and empty. It had given him such an eerie feeling that he hadn't tried anyone else.

A few outlying houses slid past, and then he was over the viaduct and into the town. There was no one in sight, but the houses looked occupied. The shops, though—most of them were closed, blind windows looked at him and he shivered.

He parked outside the A & P supermarket. It didn't look much like a store. The goods were there, but no price tags were shown and the man behind the counter did not have the air of a clerk. He was just sitting there, sitting and—thinking?

Brock went over to him, his feet curiously loud on the floor. "Uh—excuse me," he began, very softly.

The man looked up. Recognition flickered in his eyes and a brief smile crossed his face. "Oh, hello, Archie," he said, speaking with elaborate slowness. "How are you?"

"All right, thanks." Brock looked down at his shoes, unable to meet the quiet eyes. "I, well, I came to buy some stuff."

"Oh?" There was a coolness in the tone. "I'm sorry, but we aren't running things on a money basis any more."

"Well, I——" Brock squared his shoulders and forced himself to look up. "Yeah, I can see that, I guess. The national government's broken down, ain't—hasn't it?"

"Not exactly. It has just stopped mattering, that is all." The man shook his head. "We had our troubles here at the

62

beginning, but we reorganized on a rational basis. Now things are going pretty smoothly. We still lack items we could get from outside, but we can keep going indefinitely as we are, if necessary."

"A—socialist economy?"

"Well, Archie," said the man, "that's hardly the right label for it, since socialism was still founded on the idea of property. But what does ownership of a thing actually mean? It means only that you may do just what you choose with the thing. By that definition, there was very little complete ownership anywhere in the world. It was more a question of symbolism. A man said to himself, 'This is my home, my land,' and got a feeling of strength and security; because the 'my' was a symbol for that state of being, and he reacted to the symbol. Now—well—we have seen through that bit of self-deception. It served its purpose before, it made for self-respect and emotional balance, but we don't need it anymore. There's no longer any reason for binding oneself to a particular bit of soil when the economic function it served can be carried out more efficiently in other ways. So most of the farmers hereabouts have moved into town, taking over houses which were deserted by those who chose to move away from the neighborhood altogether."

"And you work the land in common?"

"Hardly the correct way to phrase it. Some of the mechanically minded have been devising machines to do most of this for us. It's amazing what can be done with a tractor engine and some junk yard scrap if you have the brains to put it together in the right way.

"We've found our level, for the time being at least. Those who didn't like it have gone, for the most part, and the rest are busy evolving new social reforms to match our new personalities. It's a pretty well-balanced setup here."

"But what do you do?"

"I'm afraid," said the man gently, "that I couldn't explain it to you."

Brock looked away again. "Well," he said finally, his voice oddly husky, "I'm all alone on the Rossman place and running short on supplies. Also, I'm gonna need help with the harvest and so on. How about it?"

"If you wish to enter our society, I'm sure a place can be found."

"No—I just want——"

"I would strongly advise you to throw in with us, Archie. You'll need the backing of a community. It isn't safe out there any more. There was a circus near here, about the time of the change, and the wild animals escaped and several of them are still running loose."

Brock felt a coldness within himself. "That must have been—exciting," he said slowly.

"It was." The man smiled thinly. "We didn't know at first, you see; we had too much of our own to worry about, and it didn't occur to us till too late that the animals were changing too. One of them must have nosed open his own cage and let out the others to cover his escape. There was a tiger hanging around town for weeks, it took a couple of children and we never did hunt it down—it just was gone one day. Where? What about the elephants and—— No, you aren't safe alone, Archie." He paused. "And then there's the sheer physical labor. You'd better take a place in our community."

"Place, hell!" There was a sudden anger in him, bleak and bitter. "All I want is a little help. You can take a share of the crop to pay for it. Wouldn't be any trouble to you if you have these fancy new machines."

"You can ask the others," said the man. "I'm not really in charge. The final decision would rest with the Council and the Societist. But I'm afraid it would be all or nothing for you, Archie. We won't bother you if you don't want us to, but you can't expect us to give you charity either. That's another outmoded symbol. If you want to fit yourself into the total economy—it's not tyrannical by any means, it's freer than any other the world has ever seen—we'll make a function for you."

"In short," said Brock thickly, "I can be a domestic animal and do what chores I'm given, or a wild one and ignored. For *my* sake—huh!" He turned on his heel. "Take it and stick it."

He was trembling as he walked out and got back into the truck. The worst of it, he thought savagely, the worst of it was that they were right. He couldn't long endure a half-in-half-out pariah status. It had been all right once, being feeble-minded; he didn't know enough then to realize what it meant. Now he did, and the dependent life would break him.

The gears screamed as he started. He'd make out without their help, damn if he wouldn't. If he couldn't be a half-tamed beggar, and wouldn't be a house pet, all right, he'd be a wild animal.

He drove back at a reckless speed. On the way, he noticed a machine out in a hayfield: a big enigmatic thing of flashing arms, doing the whole job with a single bored-looking man to guide it. They'd probably build a robot pilot as soon as they could get the materials. So what? He still had two hands.

Further along, a patch of woods came down to the edge of the road. He thought he glimpsed something in there, a great gray shape which moved quietly back out of sight, but he couldn't be sure.

His calm temperament reasserted itself as he neared the estate, and he settled down to figuring. From the cows he could get milk and butter, maybe cheese. The few hens he had been able to recapture would furnish eggs. An occasional slaughtered sheep—no, wait, why not hunt down some of those damned pigs instead?—would give him meat for quite a while; there was a smokehouse on the place. He could harvest enough hay, grain and corn—Tom and Jerry would just have to work!—to keep going through the winter; if he improvised a quern, he could grind a coarse flour and bake his own bread. There were plenty of clothes, shoes, tools. Salt was his major problem—but there ought to be a lick somewhere within a hundred miles or so, he could try to look up where and make a trip to it—and he'd have to save on gasoline and cut a lot of wood for winter, but he thought he could pull through. One way or another, he would.

The magnitude of the task appalled him. One man! One pair of hands! But it had been done before, the whole human race had come up the hard way. If he took a cut in his standard of living and ate an unbalanced diet for a while, it wouldn't kill him.

65

And he had a brain which by pre-change measures was something extraordinary. Already, he had put that mind to work: first, devising a schedule of operations for the next year or so, and secondarily inventing gadgets to make survival easier. Sure—he could do it.

He squared his shoulders and pushed down the accelerator, anxious to get home and begin.

The noise as he entered the driveway was shattering. He heard the grunts and squeals and breaking of wood, and the truck lurched with his panicky jerk at the wheel. *The pigs!* he thought. *The pigs had been watching and had seen him go—*

And he had forgotten his gun.

He cursed and came roaring up the drive, past the house and into the farmyard. There was havoc. The pigs were like small black and white tanks, chuffing and grunting. The barn door was burst open and they were in the stored feed bags, ripping them open, wallowing in the floury stuff, some of them dragging whole sacks out into the woods. There was a bull too, he must have run wild, he snorted and bellowed as he saw the man, and the cows were bawling around, they had broken down their pasture fence and gone to him. Two dead sheep, trampled and ripped, lay in the yard, the rest must have fled in terror. And Joe——

"Joe," called Brock. "Where are yuh, boy?"

It was raining a little, a fine misty downpour which blurred the woods and mingled with the blood on the earth. The old boar looked shiny as iron in the wetness. He lifted his head when the truck came and squealed.

Brock drove straight for him. The truck was his only weapon now. The boar scampered aside and Brock pulled up in front of the barn. At once the pigs closed in, battering at the wheels and sides, grunting their hate of him. The bull lowered his head and pawed the ground.

Joe barked wildly from the top of a brooder house. He was bleeding, it had been a cruel fight, but he had somehow managed to scramble up there and save himself.

Brock backed the truck, swinging it around and driving into the flock. They scattered before him, he couldn't get up enough speed in this narrow place to hit them and they weren't yielding. The bull charged.

There wasn't time to be afraid, but Brock saw death. He swung the truck about, careening across the yard, and the bull met him head on. Brock felt a giant's hand throw him against the windshield.

Ragged darkness parted before his eyes. The bull was staggering, still on his feet, but the truck was dead. The pigs seemed to realize it and swarmed triumphantly to surround the man.

He fumbled, crouched in the cab and lifting the seat. A long-handled wrench was there, comfortingly heavy. "All right," he mumbled. "Come an' get me."

Something loomed out of the woods and mist. It was gray, enormous, reaching for the sky. The bull lifted his dazed head and snorted. The pigs stopped their battering attack and for a moment there was silence.

A shotgun blast ripped like thunder. The old boar was suddenly galloping in circles, wild with pain. Another explosion sent the bull crazy, turning on his heels and making for the woods.

An elephant, gibbered Brock's mind, *an elephant come to help—*

The big gray shape moved slowly in on the pigs. They milled uneasily, their eyes full of hate and terror. The boar fell to the ground and lay gasping out his life. The elephant curled up its trunk and broke into an oddly graceful run. And the pigs fled.

Brock was still for minutes, shaking too badly to move. When he finally climbed out, the wrench hanging loosely in one hand, the elephant had gone over to the haystack and was calmly stuffing its gullet. And two small hairy shapes squatted on the ground before the man.

Joe barked feebly and limped over to his master. "Quiet, boy," mumbled Brock. He stood on strengthless legs and looked into the wizened brown face of the chimpanzee who had the shotgun.

"Okay," he said at last. The fine cold rain was chilly on his sweating face. "Okay, you're the boss just now. What do you want?"

The chimpanzee regarded him for a long time. It was a

male, he saw, the other was a female, and he remembered reading that the tropical apes couldn't stand a northern climate very well. These must be from that circus which the man in the store had spoken of, he thought, they must have stolen the gun and taken—or made a bargain with?—the elephant. Now——

The chimpanzee shuddered. Then, very slowly, always watching the human, he laid down the gun and went over and tugged at Brock's jacket.

"Do you understand me?" asked the man. He felt too tired to appreciate how fantastic a scene this was. "You know English?"

There was no answer, except that the ape kept pulling at his clothes, not hard, but with a kind of insistence. After a while, one long-fingered hand pointed from the jacket to himself and his mate.

"Well," said Brock softly, "I think I get it. You're afraid and you need human help, only you don't want to go back to sitting in a cage. Is that it?"

No answer. But something in the wild eyes pleaded with him.

"Well," said Brock, "you came along in time to do me a good turn, and you ain't killing me now when you could just as easy do it." He took a deep breath. "And God knows I could use some help on this place, you two and your elephant might make all the difference. And—and—okay. Sure."

He took off the jacket and gave it to the chimpanzee. The ape chattered softly and slipped it on. It didn't fit very well, and Brock had to laugh.

Then he straightened his bent shoulders. "All right. Fine. We'll all be wild animals together. Okay? Come along into the house and get something to eat."

CHAPTER *9*

VLADIMIR IVANOVITCH PANYUSHKIN stood under the trees, letting the rain drip onto his helmet and run off the shoulders of his coat. It was a good coat, he had taken it off a colonel after the last battle, it shed water like a very duck. The fact that his feet squelched in worn-out boots did not matter.

Vision swept down the hill, past the edge of forest and into the valley, and there the rain cut it off. Nothing stirred that he could see, nothing but the steady wash of rain, and he could hear nothing except its hollow sound. But the instrument said there was a Red Army unit in the neighborhood.

He looked at the instrument where it lay cradled in the priest's hands. Its needle was blurred with the rain that runneled across the glass dial, but he could see it dance. He did not understand the thing—the priest had made it, out of a captured radio—but it had given warning before.

"I would say they are some ten kilometers off, Vladimir Ivanovitch." The priest's beard waggled when he spoke. It was matted with rain and hung stiffly across his coarse robe. "They are circling about, not approaching us. Perhaps God is misleading them."

Panyushkin shrugged. He was a materialist himself. But if the man of God was willing to help him against the Soviet government, he was glad to accept that help. "And perhaps they have other plans," he answered. "I think we had best consult Fyodor Alexandrovitch."

"It is not good for him to be used so much, my son," said the priest. "He is very tired."

"So are we all, my friend." Panyushkin's words were toneless. "But this is a key operation. If we can cut across to Kirovograd, we can isolate the Ukraine from the rest

69

of the country. Then the Ukrainian nationalists can rise with hope of success."

He whistled softly, a few notes with a large meaning. Music could be made a language. The whole uprising, throughout the Soviet empire, depended in part on secret languages made up overnight.

The Sensitive came out of the dripping brush which concealed Panyushkin's troops. He was small for his fourteen years, and there was a blankness behind his eyes. The priest noted the hectic flush in his cheeks and crossed himself, murmuring a prayer for the boy. It was saddening to use him so hard. But if the godless men were to be overthrown at all, it would have to be soon, and the Sensitives were necessary. They were the untappable, unjammable, undetectable link which tied together angry men from Riga to Vladivostok; the best of them were spies such as no army had ever owned before. But there were still many who stood by the masters, for reasons of loyalty or fear or self-interest, and they had most of the weapons. Therefore a whole new concept of war had to be invented by the rebels.

A people may loathe their government, but endure it because they know those who protest will die. But if all the people can be joined together, to act at once—or, most of them, simply to disobey with a deadly kind of peacefulness—the government can only shoot a few. Cut off from its own strong roots, the land and the folk, a government is vulnerable and less than a million armed men may be sufficient to destroy it.

"There is a Red Star," said Panyushkin, pointing out into the rain. "Can you tell what they plan, Fyodor Alexandrovitch?"

The boy sat down on the running, sopping hillside and closed his eyes. Panyushkin watched him somberly. It was hard enough being a link with ten thousand other Sensitives across half a continent. Reaching for unlike minds would strain him close to the limit. But it had to be done.

"There is—they know us." The boy's voice seemed to come from very far away. "They—have—instruments. Their metal smells us. They—no, it is death! They send death!" He opened his eyes, sucked in a sharp gasp, and fainted. The priest knelt to take him up and cast Panyushkin a reproachful look.

"Guided missiles!" The leader whirled on his heel. "So they *do* have detectors like ours now. Good thing we checked, eh, priest? Now let us get away from here before the rockets come!"

He left enough metallic stuff behind to fool the instruments, and led his men along the ridge of hills. While the army was busy firing rockets on his camp, he would be readying an attack on their rear.

With or without the help of the priest's incomprehensible God, he felt quite sure that the attack would succeed.

Felix Mandelbaum had hardly settled into his chair when the annunciator spoke. "Gantry." The secretary's tone of voice said that it was important.

Gantry—he didn't know anybody of that name. He sighed and looked out the windows. Morning shadow still lay cool across the streets, but it was going to be a hot day.

There was a tank squatting on its treads down there, guns out to guard City Hall. The worst of the violence seemed to have passed: the Third Ba'al cult was falling apart rapidly after the prophet's ignominious capture last week, the criminal gangs were being dealt with as the militia grew in size and experience, a measure of calm was returning to the city. But there was no telling what still prowled the outer districts, and there were surely going to be other storms before everything was finally under control.

Mandelbaum sat back in his chair, forcing tensed muscles to relax. He always felt tired these days, under the thin hard-held surface of energy. Too much to do, too little time for sleep. He pushed the buzzer which signalled: Let him in.

Gantry was a tall rawboned man whose good clothes did not quite fit him. There was an upstate twang in the ill-tempered voice: "They tell me you're the dictator of the city now."

"Not exactly," said Mandelbaum, smiling. "I'm just a sort of general trouble shooter for the mayor and the council."

"Yeah. But when there's nothing but trouble, the trouble

71

shooter gets to be boss." There was a truculence in the swift reply. Mandelbaum didn't try to deny the charge, it was true enough. The mayor had all he could do handling ordinary administrative machinery; Mandelbaum was the flexible man, the co-ordinator of a thousand quarreling elements, the maker of basic policy, and the newly created city council rarely failed to vote as he suggested.

"Sit down," he invited. "What's your trouble?" His racing mind already knew the answer, but he gained time by making the other spell it out for him.

"I represent the truck farmers of eight counties. I was sent here to ask what your people mean by robbing us."

"Robbing?" asked Mandelbaum innocently.

"You know as well as I do. When we wouldn't take dollars for our stuff they tried to give us city scrip. And when we wouldn't take that, they said they'd seize our crops."

"I know," said Mandelbaum. "Some of the boys are pretty tactless. I'm sorry."

Gantry's eyes narrowed. "Are you ready to say they won't pull guns on us? I hope so, because we got guns of our own."

"Have you got tanks and planes too?" asked Mandelbaum. He waited an instant for the meaning to sink in, then went on swiftly: "Look, Mr. Gantry, there are six or seven million people left in this city. If we can't assure them a regular food supply, they'll starve. Can your association stand by and let seven million innocent men, women, and children die of hunger while you sit on more food than you can eat? No. You're decent human beings. You couldn't."

"I don't know," said Gantry grimly. "After what that mob did when it came stampeding out of the city last month——"

"Believe me, the city government did everything it could to stop them. We failed in part, the panic was too big, but we did keep the whole city from moving out on you." Mandelbaum made a bridge of his fingers and said judicially: "Now if you really were monsters you'd let the rest of them stay here to die. Only they wouldn't. Sooner or later, they'd

72

all swarm out on you, and then everything would go under."

"Sure. Sure." Gantry twisted his large red hands together. Somehow, he found himself on the defensive. "It ain't that we want to make trouble, out in the country. It's just—well, we raise food for you, but you ain't paying us. You're just taking it. Your scrip don't mean a thing. What can we buy with it?"

"Nothing, now," said Mandelbaum candidly. "But believe me, it's not our fault. The people here want to work. We just haven't got things organized enough yet. Once we do, our scrip will mean things like clothes and machinery for you. If you let us starve, though—where's your market then?"

"All that was said at the association meeting," replied Gantry. "The thing is, what guarantee have we got that you'll keep your end of the bargain?"

"Look, Mr. Gantry, we do want to co-operate. We want it so much that we're prepared to offer a representative of your people a seat on the city council. Then how can we double-cross you?"

"Hmmm—" Gantry's eyes narrowed shrewdly. "How many members on the council all told?"

They bargained for a while, and Gantry left with a city offer of four seats which would hold special veto powers on certain matters concerning rural policy. Mandelbaum was sure the farmers would accept it: it looked like a distinct victory for their side.

He grinned to himself. How do you define victory? The veto power wouldn't mean a thing, because rural policy was perfectly straightforward anyway. The city, the whole state and nation, would gain by the reunification of so large an area. Perhaps the piled-up debt to the farmers would never be paid—society was changing so rapidly that there might be no more cities in a few years—but that, however lamentable, was a small matter. What counted now was survival.

"North and Morgan," said the annunciator.

Mandelbaum braced himself. This was going to be tougher. The waterfront boss and the crazy political theorist had their own ambitions, and considerable followings

—too large to be put down by force. He stood up politely to greet them.

North was a burly man, his face hard under it· layers of fat; Morgan was slighter physically, but his eyes smoldered under the high bald forehead. They glared at each other as they came in, and looked accusingly at Mandelbaum. North growled their mutual question: "What's the idea bringing us in at the same time? I wanted to see you in private."

"Sorry," said Mandelbaum insincerely. "There must have been a mix-up. Would you mind both just sitting down for a few minutes, though? Maybe we can work it out together somehow."

"There is no 'somehow' about it," snapped Morgan. "I and my followers are getting sick of seeing the obvious principles of Dynapsychism ignored in this government. I warn you, unless you reorganize soon along sensible lines——"

North brushed him aside and turned to Mandelbaum. "Look here, there're close to a hundred ships layin' idle in the port of New York while th' East Coast and Europe're yellin' for trade. My boys're gettin' fed up with havin' their voice go unheard."

"We haven't had much word from Europe lately," said Mandelbaum in apologetic tone. "And things are too mixed up yet for us even to try coastwise trading. What'd we trade with? Where'd we find fuel for those ships? I'm sorry, but——" His mind went on: *The real trouble is, your racket hasn't got any waterfront to live off now.*

"It all comes from blind stubbornness," declared Morgan. "As I have conclusively shown, a social integration along the psychological principles I have discovered would eliminate——"

And your trouble is, you want power, and too many people are still hunting a panacea, a final answer, thought Mandelbaum coldly. *You sound intellectual, so they think you are; a certain class still wants a man on a white horse, but prefers him with a textbook under one arm. You and Lenin!*

"Excuse me," he said aloud. "What do you propose to do, Mr. North?"

"New York started as a port an' it'll be a port again before long. This time we wanna see that the workers that make the port go, get their fair share in governin' it!"

In other words, you also want to be dictator. Aloud, thoughtfully: "There may be something in what you both say. But we can't do everything at once, you know. It seems to me, though, like you two gentlemen are thinking along pretty parallel lines. Why don't you get together and present a united front? Then I'd find it a lot easier to put your proposals before the council."

Morgan's pale cheeks flushed. "A band of sweaty human machines——"

North's big fists doubled. "Watch y'r langwidge, sonny boy."

"No, really," said Mandelbaum. "You both want a better integrated government, don't you? It seems to me——"

Hmmm. The same thought lit the two pairs of eyes. It had been shockingly easy to plant it. *Together, perhaps, we could . . . and then afterward I can get rid of him*——

There was more discussion, but it ended with North and Morgan going out together. Mandelbaum could almost read their contempt for him; hadn't he ever heard of divide and rule?

Briefly, there was sadness in him. So far, people hadn't really changed much. The wild-eyed dreamer simply built higher castles in the clouds; the hard-boiled racketeer had no vocabulary of ideas or concepts to rise above his own language of greed.

It wouldn't last. Within months, there would be no more Norths and no more Morgans. The change in themselves, and in all mankind, would destroy their littleness. But meanwhile, they were dangerous animals and had to be dealt with.

He reached for the phone and called over the web operated for him alone. "Hullo, Bowers? How're you doing?—— Look, I've got the Dynapsychist and the rackets boss together. They'll probably plan a sort of fake Popular Front, with the idea of getting seats on the council and then taking over the whole show by force—palace revolution, *coup d'état,* whatever you call it.——Yeh. Alert our agents in both parties. I'll want complete reports. Then we

want to use those agents to egg them on against each other.
——Yeah, the alliance is as unstable as any I ever heard of. A little careful pushing, and they'll bury the hatchet all right—in each other. Then when the militia has mopped up what's left of the tong war, we can start our propaganda campaign in favor of common sense. ——Sure, it'll take some tricky timing, but we can swing it.——"

For a moment, as he laid the phone down, his face sagged with an old grief. He had just condemned some scores of people, most of whom were merely bewildered and misled, to death. But it couldn't be helped. He had the life and freedom of several million human beings to save—the price was not exorbitant.

"Uneasy sits the butt that bears the boss," he muttered, and looked at his appointment list. There was an hour yet before the representative from Albany arrived. That was going to be a hot one to handle. The city was breaking state and national laws every day—it had to—and the governor was outraged. He wanted to bring the whole state back under his own authority. It wasn't an unreasonable wish, but the times weren't ripe; and when they eventually were, the old forms of government would be no more important than the difference between Homoousian and Homoiousian. But it was going to take a lot of argument to convince the Albany man of that.

Meanwhile, though, he had an hour free. He hesitated for a split second between working on the new rationing system and on the plans for extending law and order to outer Jersey. Then he laid both aside in favor of the latest report on the water situation.

CHAPTER *10*

THERE was a dimness in the laboratory which made the pulsing light at the machine's heart stand out all the brighter, weirdly blue and restless between the coils and the impassive meter faces. Grunewald's face was corpse-colored as he bent over it.

"Well," he said unnecessarily, "that seems to be that."

He flicked the main switch, and the electric hum whined and the light died. For a moment he stood thoughtfully regarding the anesthesized rat within the coils. Hairlike wires ran from its shaven body to the meters over which Johansson and Lewis stood.

Lewis nodded. "Neural rate jumps up again." He touched the dials of the oscilloscope with finicking care. "And just about on the curve we predicted. You've generated an inhibitor field, all right." There would be other tests to make, detailed study, but that could be left to assistants. The main problem was solved.

Grunewald reached in with thick, oddly delicate hands and took out the rat and began extracting the probes. "Poor little guy," he murmured. "I wonder if we're doing him a favor."

Corinth, hunched moodily on a stool, looked up sharply.

"What use is intelligence to him?" pursued Grunewald. "It just makes him realize the horror of his own position. What use is it to any of us, in fact?"

"Would you go back, yourself?" asked Corinth.

"Yes." Grunewald's square blond face held a sudden defiance. "Yes, I would. It's not good to think too much or too clearly."

"Maybe," whispered Corinth, "maybe you've got something there. The new civilization—not merely its technology, but its whole value system, all its dreams and hopes

77

—will have to be built afresh, and that will take many generations. We're savages now, with all the barrenness of the savage's existence. Science isn't the whole of life."

"No," said Lewis. "But scientists—like artists of all kinds, I suppose—have by and large kept their sanity through the change because they had a purpose in life to start with, something outside themselves to which they could give all they had." His plump face flashed with a tomcat grin. "Also, Pete, as an old sensualist I'm charmed with all the new possibilities. The art and music I used to swoon over have gone, yes, but I don't appreciate good wine and cuisine the less; in fact, my perception is heightened, there are nuances I never suspected before."

It had been a strange conversation, one of a few words and many gestures and facial expressions thrown into a simultaneous discussion of technical problems:

"Well," Johansson had said, "we've got our inhibitor field. Now it's up to you neurologists to study it in detail and find out just what we can expect to happen to life on Earth."

"Uh-huh," said Lewis. "I'm not working on that just now, though, except as a kibitzer. Bronzini and MacAndrews can handle it. I'm co-opting myself into the psychological department, which is not only more interesting but of more immediate practical importance. I'll handle the neurological-cybernetic aspect of their work."

"Our old psychology is almost useless," nodded Corinth. "We're changing too much to understand our own motivations any more. Why am I spending most of my time here, when maybe I should be home helping Sheila face her adjustment? I just can't help myself, I have to explore this new field, but—— To start afresh, on a rational basis, we'll have to know something about the dynamics of man —— As for me, I'm off this baby too, now that we've actually succeeded in generating a field. Rossman wants me to work on his spaceship project as soon as he can get it organized."

"Spaceship—faster-than-light travel, eh?"

"That's right. The principle uses an aspect of wave mechanics which wasn't suspected before the change. We'll generate a psi wave which—— Never mind, I'll explain it to you when you've gotten around to learning tensor analysis and matrix algebra. I'm collaborating with some others here in drawing up plans for the thing, while we wait for the men and materials to start building. We should be able to go anywhere in the galaxy once we've got the ship."

The two threads coalesced: "Running away from ourselves," said Grunewald. "Running into space itself to escape." For a moment the four men were silent, thinking.

Corinth got to his feet. "I'm going home," he said harshly.

His mind was a labyrinth of interweaving thought chains as he went down the stairs. Mostly he was thinking of Sheila, but something whispered of Helga too, and there was a flow of diagrams and equations, a vision of chill immensity through which the Earth spun like a bit of dust. An oddly detached part of himself was coolly studying that web of thought, so that he could learn how it worked and train himself to handle his own potentialities.

Language: The men of the Institute, who knew each other, were involuntarily developing a new set of communication symbols, a subtle and powerful thing in which every gesture had meaning and the speeding brain of the listener, without conscious effort, filled in the gaps and grasped the many-leveled meaning. It was almost too efficient, you gave your inmost self away. The man of the future would likely go naked in soul as well as in body, and Corinth wasn't sure he liked the prospect.

But then there was Sheila and himself; their mutual understanding made their talk unintelligible to an outsider. And there were a thousand, a million groups throughout the world, creating their own dialects on a basis of past experience which had not been shared with all humanity. Some arbitrary language for the whole world would have to be devised.

Telepathy? There could no longer be any doubt that it existed, in some people at least. Extrasensory perception would have to be investigated when things had quieted down. There was so much to do, and life was so terribly short!

Corinth shivered. Fear of personal extinction was supposed to be an adolescent reaction; but in a sense, all men were adolescents once more, on a new plane—no, children, babies.

Well, no doubt the biologists would within the next few years find some means of leι.gthening the lifespan, prolonging it for centuries perhaps. But was that ultimately desirable?

He came out on the street and located the automobile Rossman had provided for him. *At least,* he thought wryly as he entered it, *the parking problem has been solved. No more traffic like there once was.*

Eventually, no more New York. Big cities had no real economic justification. He came from a small town, and he had always loved mountains and forests and sea. Still, there was something about this brawling, frenetic, overcrowded, hard, inhuman, magnificent city whose absence would leave an empty spot in the world to come.

It was a hot night. His shirt stuck clammily to him, and the air seemed thick. Overhead, between the darkened buildings and the dead neon signs, heat lightning flickered palely and all the earth yearned for rain. His headlights cut a dull swath through the gummy blackness.

There were more cars abroad than there had been even a week ago. The city was just about tamed now; the gang war between Portmen and Dynapsychists, suppressed two weeks back, seemed to have been the last flare of violence. Rations were still short, but people were being put to work again and they'd all live.

Corinth pulled up in the parking lot behind his apartment and walked around to the front. The power ration authority had lately permitted this building to resume elevator service, which was a mercy. He hadn't enjoyed climbing fifteen flights when electricity was really short.

I hope—— He was thinking of Sheila, but he left the thought unfinished. She'd been getting thin, poor kid, and she didn't sleep well and sometimes she woke with a dry scream in her throat and groped blindly for him. He wished his work didn't take him away from her. She needed companionship badly. Maybe he could get her some kind of job to fill the hours.

When he came out on his floor, the hall was darkened save for a vague night light, but radiance streamed under his door. Glancing at his watch, he saw that it was later than her usual bedtime. So she couldn't sleep tonight, either.

He tried the door, but it was locked and he rapped. He thought he heard a smothered scream from within, and knocked harder. She opened the door so violently that he almost fell inside.

"Pete, Pete, Pete!" She pressed herself to him with a shudder. With his arms about her, he felt how close the delicate ribs lay to her skin. The lamplight was harsh, filling the room, and oddly lusterless on her hair. When she lifted her face, he saw that it was wet.

"What's the matter?" he asked. He spoke aloud, in the old manner, and his voice was suddenly wavering.

"Nerves." She drew him inside and closed the door. In a nightgown and bathrobe she looked pathetically young, but there was something ancient in her eyes.

"Hot night to be wearing a robe," he said, groping for expression.

"I feel cold." Her lips trembled.

His own mouth fell into a harsh line, and he sat down in an easy chair and pulled her to his lap. She laid arms about him, hugging him to her, and he felt the shiver in her body.

"This is not good," he said. "This is the worst attack you've had yet."

"I don't know what I'd have done if you'd been much longer about coming," she said tonelessly.

They began to talk then, in the new interweaving of word and gesture, tone and silence and shared remembering, which was peculiarly theirs.

"I've been thinking too much," she told him. "We all think too much these days." (Help me, my dearest! I am going down in darkness and only you can rescue me.)

"You'll have to get used to it," he answered dully. (How can I help? My hands reach for you and close on emptiness.)

"You have strength——" she cried. "Give it to me!" (Nightmares each time I try to sleep. Waking, I see the world and man as a flickering in cold and nothingness,

81

empty out to the edge of forever. I can't endure that vision.)

Weariness, hopelessness: "I'm not strong," he said. "I just keep going somehow. So must you."

"Hold me close, Pete," *Father image,* "hold me close," she whimpered. Pressing to him as if he were a shield against the blackness outside and the darkness within and the things rising through it: "Don't ever let me go!"

"Sheila," he said. (Beloved: wife, mistress, comrade.) "Sheila, you've got to hang on. All this is just an increased power to think—to visualize, to handle data and the dreams you yourself have created. Nothing more."

"But it is changing *me!*" The horror of death was in her now. She fought it with something like wistfulness: "—and where has our world gone? Where are our hopes and plans and togetherness?"

"We can't bring them back," he replied. Emptiness, irrevocability: "We have to make out with what we have now."

"I know, I know—and I can't!" Tears gleamed along her cheeks. "Oh, Pete, I'm crying more for you now," (Maybe I won't even go on loving you.) "than for me."

He tried to stay cool. "Too far a retreat from reality is insanity. If you went mad——" Unthinkableness.

"I know, I know," she said. "All too well, Pete. Hold me close."

"And it doesn't help you to know——" he said, and wondered if the engineers would ever be able to find the breaking strength of the human spirit. He felt very near to giving way.

CHAPTER *11*

SUMMER waned as the planet turned toward winter. On a warm evening late in September, Mandelbaum sat by the window with Rossman, exchanging a few low-voiced words. The room was unlit, full of night. Far below them the city of Manhattan glowed with spots of radiance, not the frantic flash and glare of earlier days but the lights of a million homes. Overhead, there was a dull blue wash of luminance across the sky, flickering and glimmering on the edge of visibility. The Empire State Building was crowned with a burning sphere like a small sun come to rest, and the wandering air held a faint tingle of ozone. The two men sat quietly, resting, smoking the tobacco which had again become minutely available, Mandelbaum's pipe and Rossman's cigarette like two ruddy eyes in the twilit room. They were waiting for death.

"Wife," said Rossman with a note of gentle reproach. It could be rendered as: (I still don't see why you wouldn't tell your wife of this, and be with her tonight. It may be the last night of your lives.)

"Work, city, time," and the immemorial shrug and the wistful tone: (We both have our work to do, she at the relief center and I here at the defense hub. We haven't told the city either, you and I and the few others who know. It's best not to do so, eh?) *We couldn't have evacuated them, there would have been no place for them to go and the fact of our attempting it would've been a tip-off to the enemy, an invitation to send the rockets immediately. Either we can save the city or we can't; at the moment, there's nothing anyone can do but wait and see if the defense works.* (I wouldn't worry my Liebchen—she'd worry on my account and the kids' and grandchildren's. No, let it happen, one way or the other. Still I do wish we could

83

be together now, Sarah and I, the whole family——)
Mandelbaum tamped his pipe with a horny thumb.

(The Brookhaven men think the field will stop the blast
and radiation), implied Rossman. *We've had them working secretly for the past month or more, anticipating an
attack. The cities we think will be assailed are guarded
now—we hope.* (But it's problematic. I wish we didn't
have to do it this way.)

"What other way?" *We knew, from our spies and deduc-
tions, that the Soviets have developed their intercontinental
atomic rockets, and that they're desperate. Revolution at
home, arms and aid being smuggled in to the insurgents
from America. They'll make a last-ditch attempt to wipe
us out, and we believe the attack is due tonight. But if it
fails, they've shot their bolt. It must have taken all their
remaining resources to design and build those rockets.*
"Let them exhaust themselves against us, while the rebels
take over their country. Dictatorship is done for."

"But what will replace it?"

"I don't know. When the rockets come, it seems to me
they'll be the last gasp of animal man. Didn't you once
call the twentieth century the Era of Bad Manners? We
were stupid before—incredibly stupid! Now all that's fading away."

"And leaving—nothing." Rossman lit a fresh cigarette
and stubbed out the old one. The brief red light threw his
gaunt, fine-boned face into high relief against darkness.

"Oh, yes," he went on, "the future is not going to look
anything like the past. Presumably there will still be society—or societies—but they won't be the same kind as
those we've known before. Maybe they'll be purely abstract, mental things, interchanges and interactions on the
symbolic level. Nevertheless, there can be better or worse
societies developed out of our new potentialities, and I
think the worse ones will grow up."

"Hm." Mandelbaum drew hard on his pipe. "Aside
from the fact that we have to start from scratch, and so
are bound to make mistakes, why should that necessarily
be so? You're a born pessimist, I'm afraid."

"No doubt. I was born into one age, and saw it die in
blood and madness. Even before 1914, you could see the

world crumbling. That would make a pessimist of anyone. But I think it's true what I say. Because man has, in effect, been thrown back into utter savagery. No, not that either; the savage does have his own systems of life. Man is back on the animal plane."

Mandelbaum's gesture swept over the huge arrogance of the city. "Is that animal?"

"Ants and beavers are good engineers." *Or were. I wonder what the beavers are doing now.* "Material artifacts don't count for much, really. They're only possible because of a social background of knowledge, tradition, desire—they're symptoms, not causes. And we have had all our background stripped from us.

"Oh, we haven't forgotten anything, no. But it's no longer of value to us, except as a tool for the purely animal business of survival and comfort. Think over your own life. What use do you see in it now? What are all your achievements of the past? Ridiculous!

"Can you read any of the great literature now with pleasure? Do the arts convey anything to you? The civilization of the past, with its science and art and beliefs and meanings, is so inadequate for us now that it might as well not exist. We have no civilization any longer. We have no goals, no dreams, no creative work—nothing!"

"Oh, I don't know about that," said Mandelbaum with a hint of amusement. "I've got enough to do—to help out with, at least—for the next several years. We've got to get things started on a worldwide basis, economics, politics, medical care, population control, conservation, it's a staggering job."

"But after that?" persisted Rossman. "What will we do then? What will the next generation do, and all generations to come?"

"They'll find something."

"I wonder. The assignment of building a stable world order is herculean, but you and I realize that for the new humanity it's possible—indeed, only a matter of years. But what then? At best, man may sit back and stagnate in an unchanging smugness. A horribly empty sort of life."

"Science——"

"Oh, yes, the scientists will have a field day for a while.

But most of the physicists I've talked to lately suspect that the potential range of science is not unlimited. They think the variety of discoverable natural laws and phenomena must be finite, all to be summed up in one unified theory—and that we're not far from that theory today. It's not the sort of proposition which can ever be proved with certainty, but it looks probable.

"And in no case can we all be scientists."

Mandelbaum looked out into darkness. *How quiet the night is,* he thought. Wrenching his mind from the vision of Sarah and the children: "Well, how about the arts? We've got to develop a whole new painting, sculpture, music, literature, architecture—and forms that have never been imagined before!"

"If we get the right kind of society." (Art, throughout history, has had a terrible tendency to decay, or to petrify into sheer imitation of the past. It seems to take some challenge to wake it up again. And again, my friend, we can't all be artists either.)

"No?" (I wonder if every man won't be an artist and a scientist and a philosopher and——)

"You'll still need leaders, and stimulus, and a world symbol." (That's the basic emptiness in us today: we haven't found a symbol. We have no myth, no dream. 'Man is the measure of all things'—well, when the measure is bigger than everything else, what good is it?)

"We're still pretty small potatoes." Mandelbaum gestured at the window and the bluely glimmering sky. (There's a whole universe out there, waiting for us.)

"I think you have the start of an answer," said Rossman slowly. (Earth has grown too small, but astronomical space—it may hold the challenge and the dream we need. I don't know. All I know is that we had better find one.)

There was a thin buzz from the telecom unit beside Mandelbaum. He reached over and flipped the switch. There was a sudden feeling of weariness in him. He ought to be tense, jittering with excitement, but he only felt tired and hollow.

The machine clicked a few signals: "Space station robot reports flight of rockets from Urals. Four are due at New York in about ten minutes."

"Ten minutes!" Rossman whistled. "They must have an atomic drive."

"No doubt." Mandelbaum dialed for Shield Center in the Empire State Building. "Brace your machinery, boys," he said. "Ten minutes to go."

"How many?"

"Four. They must figure on our stopping at least three, so they'll be powerful brutes. Hydrogen-lithium warheads, I imagine."

"Four, eh? Okay, boss. Wish us luck."

"Wish *you* luck?" Mandelbaum grinned crookedly.

The city had been told that the project was an experiment in illumination. But when the blueness strengthened to a steady glow, like a roof of light, and the sirens began to hoot, everyone must have guessed the truth. Mandelbaum thought of husbands clutching wives and children to them and wondered what else might be happening. *Prayer? Not likely; if there was to be a religion in the future, it could not be the animism which had sufficed for the blind years. Exaltation in battle? No, that was another discarded myth. Wild panic? Maybe a little of that.*

Rossman had seen at least a good deal of truth, thought Mandelbaum. *There was nothing for man to do now, in the hour of judgment, except to scream with fear or to stoop over those he loved and try to shelter them with his pitiful flesh. No one could honestly feel that he was dying for something worthy. If he shook his fist at heaven, it was not in anger against evil, it was only a reflex.*

Emptiness—Yes, he thought, *I suppose we do need new symbols.*

Rossman got up and felt his way through the dusk to a cabinet where he opened a drawer and took out a bottle. "This is some '42 burgundy I've been saving," he said. (Will you drink with me?)

"Sure," said Mandelbaum. He didn't care for wine, but he had to help his friend. Rossman wasn't afraid, he was old and full of days, but there was something lost about him. To go out like a gentleman—well, that was a symbol of sorts.

Rossman poured into crystal goblets and handed one to Mandelbaum with grave courtesy. They clinked glasses and drank. Rossman sat down again, savoring the taste.

"We had burgundy on my wedding day," he said.

"Ah, well, no need to cry into it," answered Mandelbaum. "The screen will hold. It's the same kind of force that holds atomic nuclei together—nothing stronger in the universe."

"I was toasting animal man," said Rossman. (You are right, this is his last gasp. But he was in many ways a noble creature.)

"Yeah," said Mandelbaum. (He invented the most ingenius weapons.)

"Those rockets—" (They do represent something. They are beautiful things, you know, clean and shining, built with utter honesty. It took many patient centuries to reach the point where they could be forged. The fact that they carry death for us is incidental.)

(I don't agree.) Mandelbaum chuckled, a sad little sound in the great quiet around him.

There was a luminous-dialed clock in the room. Its sweep-second hand went in a long lazy circle, once around, twice around, three times around. The Empire State was a pylon of darkness against the dull blue arc of sky. Mandelbaum and Rossman sat drinking, lost in their own thoughts.

There was a glare like lightning all over heaven, the sky was a sudden incandescent bowl. Mandelbaum covered his dazzled eyes, letting the goblet fall shattering to the floor. He felt the radiance on his skin like sunshine, blinking on and off. The city roared with thunder.

—two, three, four.

Afterward there was another stillness, in which the echoes shuddered and boomed between high walls. A wind sighed down the empty streets, and the great buildings shivered slowly back toward rest.

"Good enough," said Mandelbaum. He didn't feel any particular emotion. The screen had worked, the city lived —all right, he could get on with his job. He dialed City Hall. "Hello, there. All okay? Look, we got to get busy, check any panic and——"

Out of the corner of one eye he saw Rossman sitting quietly, his unfinished drink on the arm of the chair.

CHAPTER *12*

CORINTH sighed and pushed the work from him. The murmurs of the evening city drifted faintly up to him through a window left open to the October chill. He shivered a little, but fumbled out a cigarette and sat for a while smoking.

Spaceships, he thought dully. *Out at Brookhaven they're building the first star ship.*

His own end of the project was the calculation of intranuclear stresses under the action of the drive field, a task of some complexity but not of such overreaching importance that the workers couldn't go ahead on the actual construction before he finished. He had been out there just today, watching the hull take shape, and his professional self had found a cool sort of glory in its perfected loveliness. Every organ of the ship, engine and armor and doors and ports and controls, was a piece of precision engineering such as Earth had never seen before. It was good to be a part of such work.

Only——

He swore softly, grinding out the cigarette in an overloaded ashtray and rising to his feet. It was going to be one of his bad nights; he needed Helga.

The Institute hummed around him as he went down the familiar halls. They were working on a twenty-four hour schedule now, a thousand liberated minds spreading toward a horizon which had suddenly exploded beyond imagination. He envied the young technicians. They were the strong and purposeful and balanced, the future belonged to them and they knew it. At thirty-three, he felt exhausted with years.

Helga had come back to resume directorship here: on its new basis, it was a full-time job for a normal adult, and she had the experience and the desire to serve. He thought that she drove herself too hard, and realized with a muted guilt that it was largely his fault. She never left before he did, because sometimes he needed to talk to her. This was going to be one of those times.

He knocked. The crisp voice over the annunciator said, "Come in," and he did not miss the eagerness in her voice or the sudden lighting in her eyes as he entered.

"Come have dinner with me, won't you?" he invited.

She arched her brows, and he explained hastily: "Sheila's with Mrs. Mandelbaum tonight. She—Sarah—she's good for my wife, she's got a sort of plain woman sense a man can't have. I'm at loose ends——"

"Sure." Helga began arranging her papers and stacking them away. Her office was always neat and impersonal, a machine could have been its occupant. "Know a joint?"

"You know I don't get out much these days."

"Well, let's try Rogers'. A new night club for the new man." Her smile was a little sour. "At least they have decent food."

He stepped into the small adjoining bathroom, trying to adjust his untidy clothes and hair. When he came out, Helga was ready. For an instant he looked at her, perceiving every detail with a flashing completeness undreamed of in the lost years. They could not hide from each other and—she with charasteristic honesty, he with a weary and grateful surrender—had quit trying. He needed someone who understood him and was stronger than he, someone to talk to, to draw strength from. He thought that she only gave and he only took, but it was not a relationship he could afford to give up.

She took his arm and they went out into the street. The air was thin and sharp in their lungs, it smelled of autumn and the sea. A few dead leaves swirled across the sidewalk before them, already frost had come.

"Let's walk," she said, knowing his preference. "It isn't far."

He nodded and they went down the long half-empty ways. The night loomed big above the street lamps, the cliffs of Manhattan were mountainously black around them and only a rare automobile or pedestrian went by. Corinth thought that the change in New York epitomized what had happened to the world.

"How's Sheila's work?" asked Helga. Corinth had obtained a job for his wife at the relief center, in the hope that it would improve her morale. He shrugged, not answering. It was better to lift his face into the wind that streamed thinly between the dark walls. She fell into his silence; when he felt the need for communication, she would be there.

A modest neon glow announced Rogers' Cafe. They turned in at the door, to find a blue twilight which was cool and luminous, as if the very air held a transmuted light. *Good trick,* thought Corinth, *wonder how they do it?*—and in a moment he had reasoned out the new principle of fluorescence on which it must be based. Maybe an engineer had suddenly decided he would prefer to be a restaurateur.

There were tables spaced somewhat farther apart than had been the custom in earlier times. Corinth noted idly that they were arranged in a spiral which, on the average, minimized the steps of waiters from dining room to kitchen and back. But it was a machine which rolled up to them on soft rubber wheels and extended a slate and stylus for them to write their orders on.

The menu listed few meat dishes—there was still a food shortage—but Helga insisted that the soya supreme was delicious and Corinth ordered it for both of them. There would be an aperitif too, of course.

He touched glasses with her over the white cloth. Her eyes were grave on his, waiting. *"Was hael."*

"Drinc hael," she answered. Wistfully: "I'm afraid our descendants will not understand our ancestors at all. The whole magnificent barbarian heritage will be animal mouthings to them, won't it? When I think of the future I sometimes feel cold."

"You too," he murmured, and knew that she let down her reserve only because it made it easier for him to unburden himself.

A small orchestra came out. Corinth recognized three men among them who had been famous musicians before the change. They carried the old instruments, strings and a few woodwinds and one trumpet, but there were some new ones too. Well, until philharmonic associations came back, if they ever did, no doubt serious artists would be glad of a chance to play in a restaurant—at that, they'd have a more appreciative audience than usual in the past.

His eyes went around among the customers. They were ordinary-looking people, hornyhanded laborers side by side with thin stoop-shouldered clerks and balding professors. The new nakedness had obliterated old distinctions, everybody was starting from scratch. There was an easy informality of dress, open-necked shirts, slacks and jeans, an occasional flamboyant experiment. Physical externals were counting for less every day.

There was no conductor. The musicians seemed to play extemporaneously, weaving their melodies in and out around a subtle, tacit framework. It was a chill sort of music, ice and green northern seas, a complex, compelling rhythm underlying the sigh of strings. Corinth lost himself for a while, trying to analyze it. Now and then a chord would strike some obscure emotional note within him, and his fingers tightened on the wine glass. A few people danced to it, making up their own figures as they went. He supposed that in the old days this would have been called a jam session, but it was too remote and intellectual for that. Another experiment, he thought. All humanity was experimenting, striking out after paths in a suddenly horizonless world.

He turned back to Helga, surprising her eyes as they rested on him. The blood felt hot in his face, and he tried to talk of safe things. But there was too much understanding between them. They had worked and watched together, and now there was a language of their own, every look and gesture meant something, and the meanings flickered back and forth, interlocking and breaking and meeting again, until it was like talking with one's own self.

"Work?" he asked aloud, and it meant: (How has your task been the last few days?)

"All right," she said in a flat tone. (We're accomplishing something heroic, I think. The most supremely worthwhile job of all history, perhaps. But somehow I don't care very much——)

"Glad see you tonight," he said. (I need you. I need someone in the lightless hours.)

(I will always be waiting), said her eyes.

Dangerous subject. Hide from it.

He asked quickly: "What do you think of the music here? It seems as if they're already on the track of a form suited to . . . modern man."

"Maybe so," she shrugged. "But I can still find more in the old masters. They were more human."

"I wonder if we are still human, Helga."

"Yes," she replied. "We will always remain ourselves. We will still know love and hate, fear and bravery and laughter and grief."

"But of the same kind?" he mused. "I wonder."

"You may be right," she said. "It's become too hard to believe what I want to believe. There is that."

He nodded, she smiled a little: (Yes, we both know it, don't we? That and all the world besides.)

He sighed and clenched his fists briefly: "Sometimes I wish— No." *It's Sheila I love.*

(Too late, isn't it, Pete?) said her eyes. (Too late for both of us.)

"Dance?" he invited. (Come to forgetfulness.)

"Of course." (Oh, gladly, gladly!)

They got up and moved out on the floor. He felt the strength of her as he put his arm around her waist, and it was as if he drew of it. *Mother image?* jeered his mind. No matter. The music was entering him more fully now, he felt its curious beat in his blood. Helga's head was almost level with his, but her face was hidden from him. He was not a good dancer, he let her take the lead, but the pleasure of rhythmic physical movement was sharper for him now than it had been before the change. For a moment he wished he could be a savage and dance his sorrow out before the gods.

No, too late for him. He was a child of civilization— even now; he had been born too old. But what do you do, then, when you see your wife going mad?

Ah, Love, could thou and I with Fate conspire— What a childish thing that was! And yet he had liked it once.

The music ended, and they went back to their table. The

hors d'oeuvres had arrived, borne by the machine. Corinth seated Helga and picked moodily at his dish. Presently she looked at him again.

"Sheila?" she asked: (She isn't well these days, is she?)

"No." (Thank you for asking.) Corinth grimaced. (Her work helps fill the time, but she's not good at it. She broods, and she's begun seeing things, and her dreams at night——)

Oh, my tormented dearest! "But why?" (You and I, most people, we're adjusted now, we aren't nervous any more; I always thought she was more stable than average.)

"Her subconscious mind . . ." (Running wild, and her consciousness can't control it, and worry over the symptoms only makes matters worse . . .) "She just isn't made for such power of mind, she can't handle it."

Their eyes met: *Something lost, of old innocence, all we once treasured stripped from us, and we stand naked before our own solitude.*

Helga lifted her head: (We have to face it out. Somehow we have to keep going.) *But the loneliness!*

(I'm coming to depend too much on you. Nat and Felix are wrapped up in their own work. Sheila has no strength left, she has been fighting herself too long. There's only you, and it's not good for you.)

(I don't mind.) *It's all I have, now when I can no longer hide from myself.*

Their hands clasped across the table. Then, slowly, Helga withdrew hers and shook her head.

"God!" Corinth's fists doubled. (If we could only learn more about ourselves! If we had a workable psychiatry!)

(Perhaps we will before long. It's being studied.) Soothingly: "And how is your own task coming?"

"Well enough, I suppose." (We'll have the stars within our grasp before spring. But what good is it? What use are the stars to us?) Corinth stared at his wine glass. "I'm a little drunk. I talk too much."

"No matter, darling."

He looked at her. "Why don't you get married, Helga? Find someone for yourself. You can't pull me out of my private hell."

Her face spoke negation.

94

"Better leave me out of your life," he urged in a whisper.

"Would you leave Sheila out of yours?" she asked.

The machine waiter came silently to remove their dishes and set the main course before them. Corinth thought vaguely that he ought to have no appetite. Didn't misery traditionally mean pining away? But the food tasted good. Eating—well, yes, a compensation of sorts, like drinking and daydreaming, work and anything else you cared to name.

(You have to endure) said Helga's eyes. (Whatever comes, you have to live through it, you and your sanity, because that is your heritage of humanness.)

After a while she spoke aloud, three clipped words which held an overwhelming meaning: "Pete, would you" (like to go out on the star ship?)

"Huh?" He stared at her so foolishly that she had to laugh. In a moment she spoke again, seriously and impersonally:

"It's being planned for two men." (Mostly robot-run, you know. Nat Lewis talked me into giving him one of the berths, as biologist. The problem of life elsewhere in the universe——)

His voice shook a little: "I didn't know you could control who went."

"Not officially." (In practice, since it's largely an Institute project, I can swing it for any qualified person. Nat wanted me along——) They traded a brief smile. *You could do worse, I could do better too.* "But of course a physicist is needed." (You know as much about the project, and have done as much for it, as anyone.)

"But——" He shook his head. "I'd like to——" (No, there isn't a strong enough word for it. I'd trade my chances of immortality for a berth like that. I used to lie on my back on summer nights, when I was a kid, and look at the moon rising and Mars like a red eye in heaven, and dream.) "But there's Sheila. Some other time, Helga."

"It wouldn't be a long trip," she said. (A couple of weeks' scouting around among the nearer stars, I imagine, to test out the drive and a number of astronomical theories. Nor do I think it's at all risky—would I let you go if I imagined that?) *As it is, I'll watch the sky every night and feel its great cold and clench my fists together.* (It's a chance I think you ought to have, for your own peace of mind. You're a lost soul now, Pete. You need to find something above your own problems, above this whole petty world of ours.) She smiled. "Maybe you need to find God."

"But I tell you, Sheila——"

"There's several months yet before the ship leaves." (Anything can happen in that time. I've kept in touch with the latest psychiatric research too, and there's a promising new line of treatment.) She reached over the table to touch his arm. "Think it over, Pete."

"I will," he said, a little thickly.

Part of him realized that she was holding out that tremendous prospect as an immediate diversion for him, something to break the circle of his worry and gloom. But it didn't matter. It was working anyway. When he came out again on the street with her, he looked up to the sky, saw a few suns dim through its haze, and felt a rush of excitement within him.

The stars! By Heaven, the stars!

CHAPTER *13*

SNOW fell early that year. One morning Brock came out of the house and all the world was white.

He stood for a moment looking over the sweep of land, hills and fields and buried roads, to the steel-colored dawn horizon. It was as if he had never seen winter before, bare black trees against a sky of windless quiet, burdened roofs and frost-glazed windows, and a single crow sitting dark and disconsolate on a cold telephone pole. *And indeed,* he thought, *I never have—not really.*

The snowfall had warmed the air but his breath still misted from his nostrils and he felt a tingle in his face. He slapped his hands together, a startlingly loud crack in the stillness, and blew out his cheeks and said aloud: "Well, Joe, looks like we're settled down for the next half year. White Thanksgiving, and I wouldn't be surprised if we had a white Easter too."

The dog looked up at him, understanding most of it but with little means of replying. Then instinct got the better of him and he went romping and barking to wake the farm with his clamor.

A small stocky form, so bundled up that only the proportions of arm and leg indicated it was not human, came out of the house, shuddered, and bounded quickly over to stand by the man. "Cold," she chattered. "Cold, cold, cold."

"It'll get colder, I'm afraid, Mehitabel," said Brock, and laid a hand on the chimpanzee's fur-capped head. He still feared that the apes would not last out the winter. He had tried to do what he could for them—making clothes, and assigning most of their work in the house or barn where it was warm—but still their lungs were frail.

He hoped desperately that they would live. In spite of their natural flightiness and laziness, they had labored heroically with him; he could not have readied for winter alone. But more than that, they were friends—someone to talk to, once a pidgin dialect had been worked out between him and them. They didn't have much to say, and their grasshopper minds would not stay on one subject, but they broke the solitude for him. Just to sit watching their antics in the gymnasium he had rigged up for them was to laugh, and laughter had become a rare thing.

Curiously, Mehitabel had taken best to the farmyard chores while her mate, Jimmy, handled cooking and housekeeping. Not that it mattered. They were strong and clever helpers, whatever they did.

He trudged over the yard, his boots leaving a smudge in the virginal whiteness, and opened the barn door. A wave of animal heat struck him as he entered the dimness, and the strong odor was heady. Mehitabel went to get hay and ground corn for the livestock—fifteen cows, two horses, and the vast form of Jumbo the elephant—while Brock gave himself to milking.

What stock was left seemed to have fallen into a placid

acceptance of the new order. Brock winced. They trusted him, he seemed to be a kind of informal god, and today he would have to violate their trust. No use putting it off any longer, that would only make it the more difficult.

The door creaked open again and Wuh-Wuh came lumbering in and found a milking stool and joined Brock. He said nothing, and his work went ahead mechanically, but that was not unusual. Brock imagined that Wuh-Wuh was incapable of speech, except the inarticulate stammerings and grunts which had earned him his name.

The imbecile had come tracking in one day a few weeks ago, ragged and filthy and starving. He must have escaped from some asylum—a small, knotty hunchback of uncertain age, his sloping head ugly to look on and a vacancy in his eyes. Wuh-Wuh's intelligence had, obviously, gone up like everyone else's, but that didn't change the fact that he was a defective, physically as well as mentally.

He had not been especially welcome. Most of the big tasks of harvest were done by then, and there was enough worry about supplies for winter without adding an extra mouth. "I kill him, boss," said Jimmy, reaching for a knife.

"No," said Brock. "We can't be that hard."

"I do it quick and easy," grinned Jimmy, testing the edge of the blade on one splay thumb. He had a charming jungle simplicity in him.

"No. Not yet, anyway." Brock smiled wearily. He was always tired, there was always something to do. *We're the lost sheep, and I seem to have been appointed bellwether. We all have to live in a world that don't want us.* After a moment he had added: "We need a lot of wood cut, too."

Wuh-Wuh had fitted in tolerably well, he was harmless enough once Jimmy—probably with the help of a stick— had broken him of some undesirable habits. And the business had made Brock realize with a new force that there must be many of his sort, struggling to live when civilization got too big to concern itself with them. Eventually, he supposed, the morons would have to get together somehow, establish a community and——

Well, why not admit it? He was lonely. Sometimes the depression of his loneliness was almost suicidally great. There were none of his kind to be found, not in all the wintry world, and he was working for nothing except his own unnecessary survival. He needed kinship.

He finished the milking and turned the animals out to get exercise. The water tank was frozen over, but Jumbo broke the thin crust with her trunk and they all clustered around to drink. Later in the day the elephant would have to be put to work getting more water from the emergency pump and carrying it to the tank. Jumbo looked quite shaggy now; Brock had never before realized how much hair could grow on an elephant when abrading jungle or the blowtorches of human owners didn't remove it.

He himself went over to the haystack outside the sheep fence. He had had to build a board wall around it to keep the flock from breaking through the wire and gorging themselves, but they respected his fences now. The whim of a god—— He wondered what sort of strange taboo-thoughts went on inside those narrow skulls.

Even before the change, sheep had been animals with personalities of their own, and he knew each of the forty as well as he could know any human. Bluff, quick-witted Georgina was pushing the timid Psyche away in her haste, fat old Marie Antoinette stood placidly and immovably chewing, Jo-girl did an exuberant dance all by herself in the snow—and there was the old ram, ring-horned Napoleon, magnificently regal, too conscious of supremacy to be arrogant. How could he kill one of them?

Yet there was no help for it. He and Joe and Wuh-Wuh couldn't live on hay, or even the clumsily ground flour and the apples and garden truck in the cellar; Jimmy and Mehitabel could use some broth too—and there were the hides and tallow, the very bones might be worth saving.

Only which one should it be?

He didn't like Georgina much, but she was too good to kill, he needed her blood in his future stock. Jo-girl the glad, Marie who came up and nuzzled his hand, coquettish Margy and shy Jerri and bravehearted Eleanor—which of his friends was he going to eat?

Oh, shut up, he told himself. *You made your mind up long ago.*

He whistled for Joe and opened the fence gate. The sheep looked curiously at him as they drifted from their

99

completed meal to the shed where they nested. "Get Psyche over here, Joe," he said.

The dog was off at once, leaping the drifts like coppery fire. Mehitabel came out of the chicken house and waited quietly for what she had to do. There was a knife in her hand.

Joe nudged Psyche, and the ewe looked at him with a shy sort of wonder. The dog barked, a loud clear frosty noise, and nipped her gently on the flank. She came then, plowing through the snow and out the gate. There she stood, looking up at Brock.

"Come on, girl," he said. "This way."

He closed the gate and locked it. Joe was urging Psyche around the corner of the chickenhouse, out of sight of the flock.

The pigs had been tough and clever to start with, and had moreover seen many butcherings of their own kind in earlier days. The sheep didn't know. Brock thought that if a few of their number were led off during the winter and never came back, they would merely accept the fact without worrying about it. Eventually, of course, if man was to go on living off his animals, he would have to inculcate them with some—well, religion—which demanded sacrifices.

Brock shuddered at the thought. He wasn't cut out for the role of Moloch. The human race had been sinister enough without becoming a tribe of blood-drinking gods.

"Over here, Psyche," he said.

She stood quietly looking at him. He took off his gloves and she licked his palms, her tongue warm and wet against their sweatiness. When he scratched behind her ears, she bleated very softly and moved closer to him.

Suddenly he realized the tragedy of the animals. They had never evolved for this intelligence. Man, with his hands and his speech, must have grown up as a thinking creature, he was at home with his brain. Even this sudden crushing burden of knowledge was not too great for him, because intellect had always been potentially unlimited.

But the other beasts had lived in a harmony, driven by their instincts through the great rhythm of the world, with no more intelligence than was needed for survival. They were mute, but did not know it; no ghosts haunted them, of longing or loneliness or puzzled wonder. Only now they had been thrown into that abstract immensity for which they had never been intended, and it was overbalancing them. Instinct, stronger than in man, revolted at the strangeness, and a brain untuned to communication could not even express what was wrong.

The huge indifferent cruelty of it was a gorge of bitterness in the man's throat. His vision blurred a little, but he moved with savage speed, stepping behind the sheep and throwing her down and stretching her throat out for the knife. Psyche bleated once, and he saw the horror of foreknown death in her eyes. Then the ape struck, and she threshed briefly and was still.

"Take—take—" Brock stood up. "Take her yourself, Mehitabel, will you?" He found it oddly hard to speak. "Get Wuh-Wuh t' help you. I got other things to do."

He walked slowly away, stumbling a little, and Joe and Mehitabel traded a glance of unsureness. To them, this had only been a job; they didn't know why their leader should be crying.

CHAPTER *14*

WANG KAO was hard at work when the prophet came. It was winter, and the earth lay white and stiff about the village as far as a man could see, but there would be spring again and plowing to do, and all the oxen had run off. Men and women and children would have to drag the plows, and Wang Kao desired to ease their labor as much as could be. He was ripping apart the one fuelless tractor which was the only remnant of the Communists, in search of ball bearings, when the cry rose up that a stranger was approaching across the fields.

Wang Kao sighed and laid down his work. Fumbling

through the gloom of the hut which was his smithy, he grasped his rifle and the few remaining cartridges and shrugged on a wadded blue coat. It had been a good friend, that gun, it had seen him through many hundred miles after the army broke up in mutiny and he walked home. There had still been Communist troopers loose then, to say nothing of starved folk turned bandit. Even now, one was never sure what a newcomer might be. The last stranger had come in a shining aircraft simply to bear word that there was a new government under which all men might be free; but that government was remote and feeble as yet, men had to defend themselves when the need arose.

His neighbors were waiting outside, shivering a little in the cold. Some of them had guns like his, the rest were armed only with knives and clubs and pitchforks. Their breath puffed pale from their noses. Behind their line, the women and children and old people stood in doorways, ready to dive for shelter.

Wang Kao squinted across the snow. "It is just one man," he said. "I see no weapons upon him."

"He rides a donkey, and leads another," replied his neighbor.

There was something strange here. Who had been able to manage a beast since the great change? Wang Kao felt a prickling along his neck.

It was an elderly man who neared them. He smiled kindly, and one by one the leveled guns sank. But it was odd how thinly he was clad, as if this were summer. He rode up to the line of men and greeted them in a friendly way. No one asked his errand, but the eyes that watched him were question enough.

"My name is Wu Hsi," he said, "and I have a message for you which may be of value."

"Come in, sir," invited Wang Kao, "and accept our poor hospitality. It must be bitterly cold for you."

"Why, no," said the stranger. "That is part of my message. Men need not freeze if they have no thick garments. It is all in knowing how not to freeze."

He crossed one leg over the donkey's shoulders and leaned forward. A small chill breeze ruffled his wispy gray beard. "I am one of many," he went on. "My master taught us, and now we go forth to teach others, and it is our hope that some of those we teach will themselves become prophets."

"Well, and what is it you teach, sir?" asked Wang Kao.

"It is only the proper use of the mind," replied Wu Hsi. "My master was a scholar in Fenchow, and when the great change came he saw that it was a change in men's way of thinking and set himself to search out the best ways of using his new powers. It is but a humble beginning which we have here, and yet we feel that it may be of service to the world."

"All of us can think more freely and strongly now, sir," said Wang Kao.

"Yes, I am clearly among worthy men, and yet it may be my poor words will have some newness. Think, people, how often the mind, the will, has mastered the body's weaknesses. Think how men have kept alive during sickness and famine and weariness, when no beast could do aught but die. Then think how much greater such powers must be now, if only a man can use them."

"Yes." Wang Kao bowed. "I see how you have triumphed over the chill of winter."

"There is not enough cold today to harm a man, if he but know how to keep his blood moving warmly. That is a little thing." Wu Hsi shrugged. "A heightened mind can do much with the body; I can, for instance, show you how to tell a wound to stop hurting and bleeding. But the ways of communicating with the beasts, and befriending them; the ways of remembering every tiniest thing one has ever seen or heard; the ways of having no feelings, no wishes, save those the mind says are good; the ways of talking soul to soul with another man, without ever opening the lips; the ways of thinking out how the real world must be, without blundering into vain fancies—these, I humbly feel, may be of more use to you in the long run."

"Indeed, honored sir, they would, and we are not worthy," declared Wang Kao in awe. "Will you not come in now and dine with us?"

It was a great day for the village, in spite of the news having come so quietly. Wang Kao thought that soon it would be a great day for the whole world. He wondered what the world would look like, ten years hence, and even his patient soul could hardly wait to see.

Outside the viewports, the sky was ice and darkness, a million frosty suns strewn across an elemental night. The Milky Way flowed as a river of radiance, Orion stood gigantic against infinity, and it was all cold and silence.

Space lay around the ship like an ocean. Earth's sun was dwindling as she ran outward toward endlessness, now there were only night and quiet and the titanic shining beauty of heaven. Looking at those stars, each a giant ablaze, and sensing their terrible isolation, Peter Corinth felt the soul within him quail. This was space, reaching out past imagination, worlds beyond worlds and each, in all its splendor, nothing against the mystery that held it.

"Maybe you need to find God."

Well—perhaps he had. He had at least found something more than himself.

Sighing, Corinth turned back to the metallic warmth of the cabin, grateful for finitude. Lewis sat watching the dials and chewing a dead cigar. There was nothing of awe in his round ruddy face, and he hummed a song to himself, but Corinth knew that the huge cold had reached in and touched him.

The biologist nodded ever so slightly. (Works like a charm. The psi-drive, the viewscreens, the gravity, ventilation, servomechanisms—a lovely boat we've got!)

Corinth found a chair and sat down, folding his lanky frame together and clasping his hands over one knee. Starward bound—it was a triumph, perhaps the greatest achievement of history. For it guaranteed that there would always be a history, an outwardness in man so that he could not stagnate forever on his one little planet. Only somehow he, as an individual, did not feel the exultation of conquest. This was too big for trumpets.

Oh, he had always known intellectually that the cosmos was vast beyond comprehension, but it had been a dead knowledge in him, colorless, ten to the umpteenth power quantities and nothing more. Now it was part of his self. He had lived it, and could never again be quite the same man.

Driven by a force more powerful than rockets, freed

from Einsteinian speed limits, the ship reacted against the entire mass of the universe, and when traveling faster than light did not have a velocity in the strict sense at all. Her most probable position shifted in an enigmatic way which had required a whole new branch of mathematics to describe. She generated her own internal pseudogravity field, her fuel was mass itself—any mass, broken down into energy, nine times ten to the twentieth ergs per gram. Her viewscreens, compensating for Doppler effect and aberration, showed the naked blaze of space to eyes that would never look on it unaided. She carried and sheltered and fed her cargo of frail organic tissue, and they who rode like gods knew their own mortality with a stark and somehow heart-lifting clarity.

For all that, she had an unfinished look. In the haste to complete a thousand years of work in a few months, the builders had left out much they might have installed, computers and robots which could have made the ship altogether automatic. The men aboard could calculate with their changed minds as well and as swiftly as any machine yet built, solving partial differential equations of high order just to get the proper setting for a control. There had been an almost desperate speed in the project, a vague realization that the new humanity had to find a frontier. The next ship would be different, much of the difference founded on data which the first one would bring back.

"Cosmic ray count holding pretty steady," said Lewis. The ship bristled with instruments mounted outside the hull and its protective warping fields. (I guess that kills off the solar-origin theory for good.)

Corinth nodded. The universe—at least out to the distance they had penetrated—seemed to hold a sleet of charged particles, storming through space from unknown origins to equally unknown destinations. Or did they have any definite points of departure? Maybe they were an integral part of the cosmos, like the stars and nebulae. The professional side of him wanted immensely to know.

"I think," he said, "that even the short trips we can make in this little segment of the galaxy are going to upset most of the past astrophysical theories." (We'll have to build a whole new cosmology.)

"And biology too, I'll bet," grunted Lewis. (I've been speculating on and off since the change, and now I'm inclined to think that life forms not based on carbon are possible.) "Well, we'll see."

We'll see—what a magical phrase!

Even the Solar System would need decades of exploration. The *Sheila*—man was beyond the animism of christening his works, but Corinth remained sentimental enough to think of the ship by his wife's name—had already visited the moon on a flight test; her real voyage had begun with a swing past Venus, ducking down to look at the windy, sandy hell of the poisonous surface, then a stop on Mars where Lewis went wild over some of the adaptations he found in the plant forms, and then outward. In one unbelievable week, two men had seen two planets and gone beyond them. The constellation Hercules lay astern: they meant to locate the fringes of the inhibitor field and gather data on it; then a dash to Alpha Centauri, to see if Sol's nearest neighbor had planets, and home again. All inside of a month!

It will be close to spring when I get back——

The late winter had still held Earth's northern hemisphere when they left. It had been a cold, dark morning. Low-flying clouds blew like ragged smoke under a sky of iron. The sprawling mass of Brookhaven had been almost hidden from them, blurred with snow and haze, and the city beyond was lost to sight.

There had not been many to see them off. The Mandelbaums had been there, of course, hunched into clothes gone old and shabby; Rossman's tall gaunt form was stiff on one side of them; a few friends, some professional acquaintances from the laboratories and workshops, that was all.

Helga had come, wearing an expensive fur coat, melted snow glistening like small diamonds in the tightly drawn blonde hair. Her jewel-hard coolness said much to Corinth, he wondered how long she would wait after the ship was gone to weep, but he had shaken hands with her and found no words. Thereafter she had talked with Lewis, and Corinth had led Sheila around behind the ship.

She looked small and fragile in her winter coat. Flesh

had melted from her, the fine bones stood out under the skin and her eyes were enormous. She had become so quiet lately, she sat and looked past him and now and then she trembled a little. The hands that lay in his were terribly thin.

"I shouldn't be leaving you, honey," he said, using all the words in the old manner and making his voice a caress.

"It won't be for long," she answered tonelessly. She wore no make-up, and her lips were paler than they should be. "I think I'm getting better."

He nodded. The psychiatrist, Kearnes, was a good man, a plump fatherly sort with a brain like a razor. He admitted that his therapy was experimental, a groping into the unknown darknesses of the new human mind, but he had been getting results with some patients. Rejecting the barbarity of brain mutilation by surgery or shock, he felt that a period of isolation from familiarity gave the victim a chance to perform, under guidance, the re-evaluation that was necessary. . . .

("The change has been an unprecedented psychic shock to every organism possessed of a nervous system," Dr. Kearnes had said. "The fortunate ones—the strong-willed, the resolute, those whose interests have been by choice or necessity directed outward rather than introspectively, those to whom hard thinking has always been a natural and pleasurable process—they seem to have made the adjustment without too much damage; though I suppose we will all carry the scars of that shock to our graves. But those less fortunate have been thrown into a neurosis which has in many cases become deep psychosis. Your wife, Dr. Corinth—let me be blunt—is dangerously close to insanity. Her past life, essentially unintellectual and sheltered, has given her no preparation for a sudden radical change in her own being; and the fact that she has no children to worry about, and no problem of bare survival to occupy her, enabled the whole force of realization to turn on her own character. The old adjustments, compensations, protective forgetfulness and self-deception, which we all had, are no longer of use, and she hasn't been able to find new ones. Worry about the symptoms naturally increased them, a vicious circle. But I think I can help her;

in time, when the whole business is better understood, it should be possible to effect a complete cure. . . . How long? How should I know? But hardly more than a few years, at the rate science can expand now; and meanwhile Mrs. Corinth should be able to compensate enough for happiness and balance.")

"Well——."

Sudden terror in her eyes: "Oh, Pete, darling, darling, be careful out there! Come back to me!"

"I will," he said, and bit his lip.

("Yes, it would be an excellent thing for her—I think—if you went on that expedition, Dr. Corinth. Worry about you is a healthier thing than brooding over the shadows her own runaway mind creates for her. It will help wrench her psychic orientation outward where it belongs. She's not a natural introvert. . . .")

A flurry of snow wrapped them for a moment, hiding them from the world. He kissed her, and knew that in all the years before him he would remember how cool her lips were and how they trembled under his.

There was a deep hollow ringing in the ground, as if the planet itself shuddered with cold. Overhead flared the transatlantic rocket, bound for Europe on some mission of the new-born world order. Corinth's eyes were on Sheila. He brushed the snow from her hair, feeling the softness of it and the childish inward curve of her nape under his fingers. A small sad laughter was in him.

With five words, and eyes and hands and lips, he said to her: "When I come home again—and what a homecoming that will be, honey!—I expect to find you well and inventing a robot housemaid so you'll be free for me. I don't want anything in all the universe to bother us then."

And what he meant was: *O most beloved, be there for me as You have always been, You who are all my world. Let there be no more darkness between us, child of light, let us be together as once we were, or else all time is empty forever.*

"I'll try, Pete," she whispered. Her hand reached up to touch his face. "Pete," she said wonderingly.

Lewis' voice sounded harsh around the flank of the ship, distorted by the wind: "All aboard that's going aboard!"

Corinth and Sheila took their time, and the others respected that need. When the physicist stood in the air lock waving good-by, he was well above ground, and Sheila's form was a very small shape against the muddy snow.

Sol was little more than the brightest star in their wake, almost lost in the thronging multitude of suns, out here as far as the orbit of Saturn. The constellations had not changed, for all the leagues that had fled behind them. The huge circle of the Milky Way and the far mysterious coils of the other galaxies glimmered as remotely as they had done for the first half-man who lifted his eyes skyward and wondered. There was no time, no distance, only a vastness transcending miles and years.

The *Sheila* probed cautiously ahead at well under light velocity. On the fringes of the inhibitor field Lewis and Corinth were preparing the telemetered missiles which would be shot into the region of denser flux.

Lewis chuckled with amiable diablerie at the caged rats he meant to send on one of the torpedoes. Their beady eyes watched him steadily, as if they knew. "Poor little bums," he said. "Sometimes I feel like a louse." He added with a grin, "The rest of the time I do too, but it's fun."

Corinth didn't answer. He was looking out at the stars.

"The trouble with you," said Lewis, settling his bulk into the adjoining chair, "is that you take life too seriously. You've always done so, and haven't broken the habit since the change. Now me—I am, of course, perfect by definition!—I always found things to swear about and cry over, but there was just as much which was outrageously funny. If there is a God of any kind—and since the change I'm beginning to think there may be, perhaps I've become more imaginative—then Chesterton was right in including a sense of humor among His attributes." He clicked his tongue. "Poor old G.K.C.! It's too bad he didn't live to see the change. What paradoxes he would have dreamed up!"

The alarm bell broke off his monologue. Both men started, looking at the indicator light which blinked like a red eye, on and off, on and off. Simultaneously, a wave of dizziness swept through them. Corinth grabbed for the arms of his chair, retching.

"The field—we're approaching the zone——" Lewis punched a key on the elaborate control panel. His voice was thick. "Got to get outta here——"

Full reverse! But it wasn't that simple, not when you dealt with the potential field which modern science identified with ultimate reality. Corinth shook his head, fighting the nausea, and leaned over to help. *This switch—no, the other one——*

He looked helplessly at the board. A needle crept over a red mark, they had passed light speed and were still accelerating, the last thing he had wished. *What to do?*

Lewis shook his head. Sweat gleamed on the broad face. "Sidewide vector," he gasped. "Go out tangentially——"

There were no constants for the psi-drive. Everything was a variable, a function of many components depending on the potential gradients and on each other. The setting for "ahead" could become that for "reverse" under new conditions, and there was the uncertainty principle to reckon with, the uncaused chaos of individual electrons, flattened probability curves, the unimaginable complexity which had generated stars and planets and thinking humans. A train of equations gibbered through Corinth's brain.

The vertigo passed, and he looked at Lewis with a growing horror. "We were wrong," he mumbled. "The field builds up quicker than we thought."

"But—it took days for Earth to get out of it altogether, man, at a relative speed of——"

"We must have hit a different part of the cone, then, a more sharply defined one; or maybe the sharpness varies with time in some unsuspected manner——" Corinth grew aware that Lewis was staring at him, openmouthed.

"Huh?" said the other man—how slowly!

"I said—what did I say?" Corinth's heart began thundering in his panic. He had spoken three or four words, made a few signs, but Lewis hadn't understood him.

Of course he hadn't! They weren't as bright as they had been, neither of them.

Corinth swallowed a tongue that seemed like a piece of wood. Slowly, in plain English, he repeated his meaning.

"Oh, yes, yes." Lewis nodded, too frozen to say more.

Corinth's brain felt gluey. There was no other word. He was spiraling down into darkness, he couldn't think, with every fleeting second he tumbled back toward animal man.

The knowledge was like a blow. They had plunged unawares into the field Earth had left, it was slowing them down, they were returning to what they had been before the change. Deeper and deeper the ship raced, into an ever stronger flux, and they no longer had the intelligence to control her.

The next ship will be built to guard against this, he thought in the chaos. *They'll guess what's happened—but what good will that do us?*

He looked out again; the stars wavered in his vision. *The field,* he thought wildly, *we don't know its shape or extent. I think we're going out tangentially, we may come out of the cone soon—or we may be trapped in here for the next hundred years.*

Sheila!

He bowed his head, too miserable with the physical torment of sudden cellular readjustment to think any more, and wept.

The ship went on into darkness.

CHAPTER *15*

THE house stood on Long Island, above a wide strand sloping to the sea. It had once belonged to an estate, and there were trees and a high wall to screen it off from the world.

Roger Kearnes brought his car to a halt under the portico and stepped out. He shivered a little and jammed his hands into his pockets as the raw wet cold fell over him. There was no wind, no shadow, only the late fall of snow, thick sad snow that tumbled quietly from a low sky and clung to the windowpanes and melted on the ground like tears. He wondered despairingly if there would ever again be a springtime.

Well— He braced himself and rang the doorbell. There was work to do. He had to check up on his patient.

Sheila Corinth opened the door for him. She was still thin, her eyes dark and huge in the pale childlike face; but she wasn't trembling any more, and she had taken the trouble to comb her hair and put on a dress.

"Hello, there," he said, smiling. "How are you today?"

"Oh—all right." She didn't meet his eyes. "Won't you come in?"

She led the way down a corridor whose recent repainting had not quite succeeded in creating the cheerful atmosphere Kearnes wanted. But you couldn't have everything. Sheila could consider herself lucky to have an entire house and a pleasant elderly woman—a moron—for help and companionship. Even nowadays, it meant a lot if your husband was an important man.

They entered the living room. A fire crackled on the hearth, and there was a view of beach and restless ocean. "Sit down," invited Sheila listlessly. She threw herself into an armchair and sat unmoving, her eyes fixed on the window.

Kearnes' gaze followed hers. How heavily the sea rolled! Even indoors, he could hear it grinding against the shore, tumbling rocks, grinding away the world like the teeth of time. It was gray and white to the edge of the world, white-maned horses stamping and galloping, how terribly loud they neighed!

Pulling his mind loose, he opened his briefcase. "I have some more books for you," he said. "Psychological texts. You said you were interested."

"I am. Thank you." There was no tone in her voice.

"Hopelessly outdated now, of course," he went on. "But they may give you an insight into the basic principles. You have to see for yourself what your trouble is."

"I think I do," she said. "I can think more clearly now. I can see how cold the universe is and how little we are——" She looked at him with fright on her lips. "I wish I didn't think so well!"

112

"Once you've mastered your thoughts, you'll be glad of this power," he said gently.

"I wish they would bring back the old world," she said.

"It was a cruel world," he answered. "We're well off without it."

She nodded. He could barely hear her whisper: "O soldier, lying hollow on the rime, there is frost in your hair and darkness behind your eyes. Let there be darkness." Before he had time for a worried frown, she continued aloud, "But we loved and hoped then. There were the little cafes, do you remember, and people laughing in twilight, there were music and dancing, beer and cheese sandwiches at midnight, sailboats, leftover pies, worrying about income taxes, our own jokes, there were the two of us. Where is Pete now?"

"He'll be back soon," said Kearnes hastily. No use reminding her that the star ship was already two weeks overdue. "He's all right. It's you we have to think about."

"Yes." She knotted her brows together, earnestly. "They still come to me. The shadows, I mean. Words out of nowhere. Sometimes they almost make sense."

"Can you say them to me?" he asked.

"I don't know. This house is on Long Island, long island, longing island, island of longing, where is Pete?"

He relaxed a trifle. That was a more obvious association than she had sprung on him last time. What had it been? *But when the uttermost hollow-frozen and time so dark that lightlessness is a weight is, then tell me, what lies beneath it.* . . . Maybe she was healing herself in the quiet of her aloneness.

He couldn't be sure. Things had changed too much. A schizophrenic's mind went into lands where he could not follow, the new patterns had simply not been mapped yet. But he thought Sheila was acting a little more healthily.

"I shouldn't play with them, I know," she said abruptly. "That's dangerous. If you take them by the hand they'll let you guide them for a while, but they won't let go of your hand again."

"I'm glad you realize that," he said. "What you want to do is exercise your mind. Think of it as a tool or a
113

muscle. Go through those drills I gave you on logical processes and general semantics."

"I have." She giggled. "The triumphant discovery of the obvious."

"Well," he laughed, "you're back on your feet enough to make snide remarks, at least."

"Oh, yes." She picked at a thread in the upholstery. "But where is Pete?"

He evaded the question and put her through some routine word-association tests. Their diagnostic value was almost nil—every time he tried them, the words seemed to have taken on different connotations—but he could add the results to his own data files. Eventually he would have enough material to find an underlying pattern. This new n-dimensional conformal-mapping technique looked promising, it might yield a consistent picture.

"I have to go," he said at last. He patted her arm. "You'll be all right. Remember, if you ever want help, or just company, in a hurry, all you have to do is call me."

She didn't get up, but sat there watching him till he was out of the door. Then she sighed. *I do not like you, Doctor Fell,* she thought. *You look like a bulldog that snapped at me once, many hundred years ago. But you're so easy to fool!*

An old song ran through her head:

> "He is dead and gone, lady,
> He is dead and gone;
> At his head a grass green turf,
> At his heels a stone."

No, she said to the other one who sang in her head. *Go away.*

The sea growled and grumbled, and snow fell thicker against the windows. She felt as if the world were closing in on her.

"Pete," she whispered. "Pete, honey, I need you so much. Please come back."

CHAPTER *16*

THEY flashed out of the field, and the next few minutes were dreadful. Then:

"Where are we?"

The unknown constellations glittered around them, and the silence was so enormous that their own breathing was loud and harsh in their ears.

"I don't know," groaned Lewis. "And I don't care. Lemme sleep, will you?"

He stumbled across the narrow cabin and flopped into a bunk, shaking with wretchedness. Corinth watched him for a moment through the blur that was his own vision, and then turned back to the stars.

This is ridiculous, he told himself sharply. *You're free again. You have the full use of your brain once more. Then use it!*

His body shuddered with pain. Life wasn't meant for changes like this. A sudden return to the old dimness, numb days fading into weeks while the ship hurled herself uncontrollably outward, and then the instant emergence, clear space and the nervous system flaring up to full intensity—it should have killed them.

It will pass, it will pass, but meanwhile the ship is still outward bound, Earth lies farther behind with every fleeting second. Stop her!

He sat grasping the arms of his chair, fighting down the dry nausea.

Calmness, he willed, *slowness, brake the racing heart, relax muscles that jerked against their bones, bank the fires of life and let them build up slowly as they should.*

He thought of Sheila waiting for him, and the image was a steadiness in his whirling universe. Gradually, he felt the strength spreading as he willed it. It was a conscious battle to halt the spasmodic gasps of his lungs, but when that was won the heart seemed to slow of itself. The retching passed away, the trembling stopped, the eyes cleared, and Peter Corinth grew fully aware of himself.

He stood up, smelling the sour reek of vomit in the cabin and activating the máchine which cleaned the place up. Looking out the viewscreens, he gathered in the picture of the sky. The ship would have changed speed and direction many times in her blind race through heaven, they could be anywhere in this arm of the galaxy, but——

Yes, there were the Magellanic Clouds, ghosts against night, and that hole of blackness must be the Coal Sack, and then the great nebula in Andromeda—Sol must lie approximately in that direction. About three weeks' journey at their top pseudospeed; then, of course, they'd have to cast about through the local region to find that very ordinary yellow dwarf which was man's sun. Allow a few days, or even a couple of weeks, for that. Better than a month!

No help for it, however impatient he was. Emotion was, causally, a psychophysiological state, and as such ought to be controllable. Corinth willed the rage and grief out of himself, willed calmness and resolution. He went over to the controls and solved their mathematical problem as well as he could with the insufficient data available. A few swift movements of his hands brought the ship's flight to a halt, turned her about, and plunged her toward Sol.

Lewis was unconscious, and Corinth didn't wake him. Let him sleep off the shock of readjustment. The physicist wanted a little privacy for thinking anyway.

He thought back over the terrible weeks in the field. When they had been there, he and Lewis, their lives since Earth had left it had seemed dreamlike. They could hardly imagine what they had been doing; they could not think and feel as those other selves had done. The chains of reasoning which had made the reorganization of the world and the building of the ship possible within months, had been too subtle and ramified for animal man to follow. After a while, their talk and their desperate scheming had

116

faded into an apathy of despair, and they waited numbly for chance to release them or kill them.

Well, thought Corinth on the edge of a mind that was dealing with a dozen things at once, *as it happened, we were released.*

He sat looking out at the stupendous glory of heaven, and the realization that he was bound home and still alive and sane was a pulse of gladness within him. But the new coolness which he had willed into himself overlay him like armor. He could throw it off at the proper time, and would, but the fact of it was overwhelming.

He should have foreseen that this would come. Doubtless many on Earth had already discovered it for themselves but, with communications still fragmentary, had not yet been able to spread the word. The history of man had, in one sense, represented an unending struggle between instinct and intelligence, the involuntary rhythm of organism and the self-created patterns of consciousness. Here, then, was the final triumph of mind.

For him it had come suddenly, the shock of re-emergence into full neural activity precipitating the change which had been latent in him. For all normal humanity, though, it must come soon—gradually, continuously, perhaps, but soon.

The change in human nature and human society which this would bring about was beyond even his imagination. A man would still have motivations, he would still want to do things, but he could select his own desires, consciously. His personality would be self-adjusted to the intellectually conceived requirements of his situation. He would not be a robot, no, but he would not resemble what he had been in the past. As the new techniques were fully worked out, psychosomatic diseases would vanish and even organic troubles ought to be controllable in high degree by the will; no more pain; every man could learn enough medicine to take care of the rest, and there would be no more doctors.

Eventually—no more death?

No, probably not that. Man was still a very finite thing. Even now, he had natural limitations, whatever they might be. A truly immortal man would eventually be smothered

117

under the weight of his own experience, the potentialities of his nervous system would be exhausted.

Nevertheless, a life span of many centuries ought to be attainable; and the specter of age, the slow disintegration which was senility, could be abolished.

Protean man—intellectual man—infinity!

The star was not unlike Sol—a little bigger, a little redder, but it had planets and one of them was similar to Earth. Corinth sent the ship plunging into the atmosphere of the night side.

Detectors swept the area. No radiation above the normal background count, that meant no atomic energy; but there were cities in which the buildings themselves shone with a cool light, and machines and radio and a world-wide intercourse. The ship recorded the voices that talked through the night, later on the language could perhaps be analyzed.

The natives, seen and photographed in a fractional second as the ship went noiselessly overhead, were of the humanoid sort, mammalian bipeds, though they had greenish fur and six fingers to a hand and altogether unhuman heads. Thronging their cities, they were almost pathetically like the crowds in old New York. The form was alien, but the life and its humble desires were the same.

Intelligence, another race of minds, man is not alone in the hugeness of space-time—once it would have marked an epoch. Now it merely confirmed a hypothesis. Corinth rather liked the creatures that walked beneath him, he wished them well, but they were only another species of the local fauna. Animals.

"They seem to be a lot more sensible than we were in the old days," said Lewis as the ship spiraled over the continent. "I see no evidence of war or preparations for war; maybe they outgrew that even before they achieved machine technology."

"Or maybe this is the planet-wide universal state," answered Corinth. "One nation finally knocked out all the others and absorbed them. We'll have to study the place a bit to find out, and I, for one, am not going to stop now to do it."

Lewis shrugged. "I daresay you're justified. Let's go,

then—a quick sweep around the day side, and we'll let it go at that."

Despite the self-command which had been growing in him, Corinth had to battle down a fury of impatience. Lewis was right in his insistence that they at least investigate the stars which lay near their homeward path. It wouldn't kill anyone on Earth to wait a few weeks more for their return, and the information would be valuable.

A few hours after entering the atmosphere, the *Sheila* left it again and turned starward. The planet fell rapidly behind her driving hull, the sun dwindled and was lost, a whole living world—life, evolution, ages of history, struggle and glory and doom, dreams, hates and fears, hope and love and longing, all the many-layered existence of a thousand million sentient beings—was swallowed by darkness.

Corinth looked out and let the shiver of dismay run free within him. The cosmos was too big. No matter how swiftly men fled through it, no matter how far they ranged in all ages to come and how mightily they wrought, it would be the briefest glimmer in one forgotten corner of the great silence. This single dust mote of a galaxy was so inconceivably huge that even now his mind could not encompass the knowledge; even in a million years, it could not be fully known; and beyond it and beyond it lay shining islands of stars, outwardness past imagination. Let man reach forth till the cosmos itself perished, he would still accomplish nothing against its unheeding immensity.

It was a healthy knowledge, bringing a humility which the coldness of his new mind lacked. And it was good to know that there would always be a frontier and a challenge; and the realization of that chill hugeness would draw men together, seeking each other for comfort, it might make them kinder to all life.

Lewis spoke slowly in the quiet of the ship: "This makes nineteen planets we've visited, fourteen of them with intelligent life."

Corinth's memory went back over what he had seen, the mountains and oceans and forests of whole worlds, the life which blossomed in splendor or struggled only to live, and the sentience which had arisen to take blind nature in hand. It had been a fantastic variety of shape and civilization. Leaping, tailed barbarians howled in their swamps; a frail and gentle race, gray like silver-dusted lead, grew their big flowers for some unknown symbolic reason; a world smoked and blazed with the fury of nations locked in an atomic death clutch, pulling down their whole culture in a voluptuous hysteria of hate; beings of centaur shape flew between the planets of their own sun and dreamed of reaching the stars; the hydrogen-breathing monsters dwelling on a frigid, poisonous giant of a planet had evolved three separate species, so vast were the distances between; the world-civilization of a biped folk who looked almost human had become so completely and inflexibly organized that individuality was lost, consciousness itself was dimming toward extinction as antlike routine took the place of thought; a small snouted race had developed specialized plants which furnished all their needs for the taking, and settled down into a tropical paradise of idleness; one nation, of the many on a ringed world, had scorned wealth and power as motivations and given themselves to a passionate artistry. Oh, they had been many and strange, there was no imagining what diversity the universe had evolved, but even now Corinth could see the pattern.

Lewis elaborated it for him: "Some of those races were much older than ours, I'm sure. And yet, Pete, none of them is appreciably more intelligent than man was before the change. You see what it indicates?"

"Well, nineteen planets—and the stars in this galaxy alone number on the order of a hundred billion, and theory says most of them have planets— What kind of a sample is that?"

"Use your head, man! It's a safe bet that under normal evolutionary conditions a race only gets so intelligent and then stops. None of those stars have been in the inhibitor field, you know.

"It ties in; it makes good sense. Modern man is not essentially different from the earliest Homo sapiens, either. The basic ability of an intelligent species is that of adapting environment to suit its own needs, rather than adapting itself to environment. Thus, in effect, the thinking race
120

can maintain fairly constant conditions. It's as true for an Eskimo in his igloo as it is for a New Yorker in his air-conditioned apartment; but machine technology, once the race stumbles on to it, makes the physical surroundings still more constant. Agriculture and medicine stabilize the biological environment. In short—once a race reaches the intelligence formerly represented by an average I.Q. of 100 to, say, 150, it doesn't need to become smarter than it is."

Corinth nodded. "Eventually surrogate brains are developed, too, to handle problems the unaided mind couldn't deal with," he said. "Computers, for instance; though writing is really the same principle. I see your point, of course."

"Oh, there's more to it than that," added Lewis. "The physical structure of the nervous system imposes limitations, as you well know. A brain can only get so big, then the neural paths become unmanageably long. I'll work out the detailed theory when I get home, if somebody else hasn't beaten me to it.

"Earth, of course, is a peculiar case. The presence of the inhibitor field made terrestrial life change its basic biochemistry. We have our structural limitations too, but they're wider because of that difference in type. Therefore, we may very well be the smartest race in the universe now —in this galaxy, at least."

"Mmmmm, maybe so. Of course, there were many other stars in the field too."

"And still are. New ones must be entering it almost daily. Lord, how I pity the thinking races on those planets! They're thrown back to a submoronic level—a lot of them must simply die out, unable to survive without minds. Earth was lucky; it drifted into the field before intelligence had appeared."

"But there must be many planets in a similar case," urged Corinth.

"Well, possibly," conceded Lewis. "There may well be races which emerged, and shot up to our present level, thousands of years ago. If so, we'll meet them eventually, though the galaxy is so big that it may take a long time. And we'll adjust harmoniously to each other." He smiled wryly. "After all, pure logical mind is so protean, and the merely physical will become so unimportant to us, that we'll

121

doubtless find those beings to be just like ourselves—whatever their bodies resemble. How'd you like to be a partner of a—a giant spider, maybe?"

Corinth shrugged. "I'd have no objections."

"No, of course not. Be fun to meet them. And we won't be alone in the universe any more——" Lewis sighed. "Still, Pete, let's face it. Only a very tiny minority of all the sentient species there must be in the galaxy can have been as fortunate as us. We may find a dozen kindred races, or a hundred—no large number. Our sort of mind is very lonely."

His eyes went out to the stars. "Nevertheless, it may be that that uniqueness has its compensations. I think I'm beginning to see an answer to the real problem: what is superbrained man going to do with his powers, what can he find worthy of his efforts? I still wonder if perhaps there hasn't been a reason—call it God—for all this to happen."

Corinth nodded absently. He was straining ahead, peering into the forward viewscreen as if his vision could leap light-years and find the planet called Earth.

CHAPTER *17*

SPRING had come late, but now there was warmth in the air and a mist of green on the trees. It was too nice a day to sit in an office, and Mandelbaum regretted his own eminence. It would be more fun to go out and shoot some golf, if the nearest course was dry enough yet. But as chief administrator of the area including roughly the old states of New York, New Jersey, and New England, he had his duties.

Well, when they had gotten the weather-turning force-screens into full production, he'd move his headquarters out in the country somewhere and sit in the open. Till then, he remained in the city. New York was dying, it had no more economic or social purpose and every day some hundreds of people left it, but the location was still convenient.

He entered the office, nodded at the staff, and went into his own sanctum. The usual stack of reports waited, but he had barely gotten started when the phone rang. He swore as he picked it up—must be rather urgent if his secretary had bucked it on to him. "Hello," he snapped.

"William Jerome." It was the voice of the superintendent of the Long Island food-factory project. He had been a civil engineer before the change and continued his old work on a higher level. "I need advice," he continued, "and you seem to be the best human-relations idea-man around."

He spoke a little awkwardly, as did Mandelbaum; both were practicing the recently developed Unitary language. It had a maximal logic and a minimal redundancy in its structure, there was a universe of precise meaning in a few words, and it would probably become the international tongue of business and science if not of poetry; but it had only been made public a week before.

Mandelbaum frowned. Jerome's work was perhaps the most important in the world today. Somehow two billion people must be fed, and the food synthesis plants would permit free distribution of an adequate if unexciting diet; but first they had to be built. "What is it this time?" he asked. "More trouble with Fort Knox?" Gold was an industrial metal now. valued for its conductivity and inertness, and Jerome wanted plenty of it for bus bars and reaction vats.

"No, they've finally begun delivering. It's the workmen. I've got a slowdown on my hands, and it may become a strike."

"What for? Higher wages?" Mandelbaum's tone was sardonic. The problem of money was still not quite solved, and wouldn't be until the new man-hour credit standard got world-wide acceptance; meanwhile he had established his own local system, payment in scrip which could be exchanged for goods and services. But there was only so much to go around: more money would be a valueless gesture.

123

"No, they've got over that. But the thing is, they don't want to work six hours a day. It's pretty dull, driving nails and mixing concrete. I've explained that it'll take time to build robots for that sort of work, but they want the leisure immediately. What am I going to do if everybody'd rather accept a minimum standard of living and sit around arguing philosophy in his off hours?"

Mandelbaum grinned. "Leisure time is part of the standard of living too. What you got to do, Bill, is make 'em want to stay on the job."

"Yeah—how?"

"Well, what's wrong with setting up loudspeakers giving lectures on this and that? Better yet, give every man a buttonhole receiver and let him tune in on what he wants to hear: talks, symphonies, or whatever. I'll call up Columbia and get 'em to arrange a series of beamcasts for you."

"You mean broadcasts, don't you?"

"No. Then they'd stay at home and listen. This series will run during working hours and be beamed exclusively at your construction site."

"Hmmm—" Jerome laughed. "It might work at that!"

"Sure. You find out what the boys want and let me know. I'll take care of the rest."

When the engineer had hung up, Mandelbaum stuffed his pipe and returned to his papers. He wished all his headaches could be fixed as easily as that. But this matter of relocation. Everybody and his dog, it seemed, wanted to live out in the country; transportation and communication were no longer isolating factors. That would involve a huge labor of transference and landscaping, to say nothing of clearing ownership titles. He couldn't resist so strong a demand, but he couldn't do it at once, either. Then there was the business of——

"O'Banion," said the annunciator.

"Hm? Oh, yes. He had an appointment, didn't he? Send him in."

Brian O'Banion had been an ordinary cop before the change; during the chaotic period he had worked with the civil police; now he was local chief of Observers. For all that, he was still a big red-faced Irishman, and it was incongruous to hear crisp Unitary coming from his mouth.

"I need some more men," he said. "The job's getting too large again."

Mandelbaum puffed smoke and considered. The Observers were his own creation, though the idea had spread far and would probably be adopted by the international government before long. The smooth operation of society required a steady flow of information, a fantastically huge amount to be correlated every day if developments were not to get out of hand. The Observers gathered it in various ways: one of the most effective was simply to wander around in the guise of an ordinary citizen, talking to people and using logic to fill in all the implications.

"Takes a while to recruit and train 'em, Brian," said Mandelbaum. "What exactly do you want them for?"

"Well, first, there's this business of the feeble-minded. I'd like to put a couple of extra men on it. Not an easy job; there are still a lot of 'em wandering around, you know, and they've got to be located and unobtrusively guided the right way, toward one of the little colonies that're springing up."

"And the colonies themselves ought to be watched more closely and guarded against interference—yeah. Sooner or later, we're going to have to decide just what to do about them. But that'll be part and parcel of what we decide to do about ourselves, which is still very much up in the air. Okay, anything else?"

"I've got a lead on—something. Don't know just what, but I think it's big and I think part of it is right here in New York."

Mandelbaum turned impassive. "What's that, Brian?" he asked quietly.

"I don't know. It may not even be criminal. But it's big. I have tips from half a dozen countries around the world. Scientific equipment and materials are going into devious channels and not being seen again—publicly."

"So? Why should every scientist give us a step-by-step account of his doings?"

"No reason. But for instance, the Swedish Observer corps tracked one thing. Somebody in Stockholm wanted a certain kind of vacuum tube, a very special kind. The manufacturer explained that his whole stock, which was very small because of the low demand, had been bought by someone else. The would-be purchaser looked up the someone else, who turned out to be an agent buying for a fourth party he'd never seen. That got the Observers interested, and they checked every lab in the country; none of them had bought the stuff, so it was probably sent out by private plane or the like. They asked the Observers in other countries to check. It turned out that our customs men had noted a caseful of these same tubes arriving at Idlewild. That put a bee in my bonnet, and I tried to find where those tubes had gone. No luck—the trail ended there.

"So I started asking Observers around the world myself, and found several similar instances. Spaceship parts vanishing in Australia, for example, or a load of uranium from the Belgian Congo. It may not mean anything at all, but, well, if it's a legitimate project, why all this secrecy? I want some more men to help me follow up on it. I don't like the smell of it."

Mandelbaum nodded. Something like a crazy, unsafe experiment in nucleonics—it could devastate his whole territory. Or there might be a more deliberate plan. No telling as yet.

"I'll see you get them," he said.

CHAPTER *18*

EARLY SUMMER: the first shy green of leaves has become a fullness enchanted with sunlight, talking with wind; it has rained just an hour ago, and the light cool wind shakes down a fine sparkle of drops, like a ghostly kiss on your uplifted face; a few sparrows dance on the long, empty streets; the clean quiet mass of the buildings is sharp against a luminous blue sky, the thousand windows catch the morning sun and throw it back in one great dazzle.

The city had a sleeping look. A few men and women walked between the silent skyscrapers; they were casually dressed, some almost nude, and the driven feverish hurry of old days was gone. Now and then a truck or automobile purred down the otherwise bare avenue. They were all running off the new powercast system, and the smokeless, dustless air was almost cruelly brilliant. There was something of Sunday about this morning, though it was midweek.

Sheila's heels tapped loudly on the sidewalk. The staccato noise jarred at her in the stillness. But she could only muffle it by slowing her pace, and she didn't want to do that. She couldn't.

A troop of boys, about ten years old, came out of the deserted shop in which they had been playing and ran down the street ahead of her. Young muscles still had to exercise, but it was saddening to her that they weren't shouting. Sometimes she thought that the children were the hardest thing to endure. They weren't like children any more.

It was a long walk from the depot to the Institute, and she could have saved her energy—for what?—by taking the subway. But the thought of being caged in metal with the new men of Earth made her shiver. It was more open and free aboveground, almost like being in the country. The city had served its day, now it was dying, and the bare blind walls around her were as impersonal as mountains. She was alone.

A shadow ran along the street, as if cast by a cloud traveling swiftly overhead. Looking up, she saw the long metallic shape vanish noiselessly behind the skyscrapers. Perhaps they had mastered gravity. What of it?

She passed by two men who were sitting in a doorway, and their conversation floated to her through the quiet:

"—starvish esthetics-the change."

Swift flutter of hands.

"*Wiedersehen.*" Sigh.

"Negate: macrocosm, un-ego, entropy. Human-meaning."

She went on a little faster.

The Institute building looked shabbier than the Fifth Avenue giants. Perhaps that was because it was still intensely in use; it did not have their monumental dignity of death. Sheila walked into the lobby. There was no one around, but an enigmatic thing of blinking lights and glowing tubes murmured to itself in a corner. She went over to the elevator, hesitated, and turned off for the staircase. No telling what they had done to the elevator—maybe it was wholly automatic, maybe it responded directly to thought commands, maybe they had a dog running it.

On the seventh floor, breathing a little sharply, she went down the corridor. It hadn't changed, at least—the men here had had too much else to do. But the old fluorescent tubes were gone, now the air itself—or the walls, ceiling, floor?—held light. It was peculiarly hard to gauge distances in that shadowless radiance.

She paused before the entrance to Pete's old laboratory, swallowing a gulp of fear. *Stupid,* she told herself, *they're not going to eat you. But what have they done inside? What are they doing now?*

Squaring her shoulders, she knocked on the door. There was a barely perceptible hesitation, then: "Come in." She turned the knob and entered.

The place had hardly changed at all. That was perhaps the most difficult thing to understand. Some of the apparatus was standing in a corner, dusty with neglect, and she did not comprehend the thing which had grown up to cover three tables. But it had always been that way when she visited her husband in the old days, a clutter of gadgetry that simply didn't register on her ignorance. It was still the same big room, the windows opened on a heartlessly bright sky and a remote view of docks and warehouses, a shabby smock hung on the stained wall, and a faint smell of ozone and rubber was in the air. There were still the worn reference books on Pete's desk; his table-model cigarette lighter—she had given it to him for Christmas, oh, very long ago—was slowly tarnishing by an empty ash tray, the chair was shoved back a little as if he had only gone out for a minute and would return any time.

Grunewald looked up from the thing on which he

worked, blinking in the nearsighted manner she recalled. He looked tired, his shoulders stooped more than they once did, but the square blond face was the same. A dark young man whom she didn't know was helping him.

He made a clumsy gesture. (Why, Mrs. Corinth! This is an unexpected pleasure. Do come in.)

The other man grunted and Grunewald waved at him. (This is) "Jim Manzelli," he said. (He's helping me out just now. Jim, this is) "Mrs. Corinth," (wife of my former boss).

Manzelli nodded. Curtness: (Pleased to meet you.) He had the eyes of a fanatic.

Grunewald went over to her, wiping grimy hands. "Why" (are you here, Mrs. Corinth)?

She answered slowly, feeling her timidity harsh in her throat. (I only wanted to) "Look around." (I) "Won't bother" (you very) "long." Eyes, fingers twisting together: Plea for kindness.

Grunewald peered more closely at her, and she saw the expressions across his face. Shock: *You have grown so thin! There is something haunted about you, and your hands are never still.* Compassion: *Poor girl, it's been hard for you, hasn't it? We all miss him.* Conventional courtesy: (I hope you are over your) "Illness?"

Sheila nodded. (Where is) "Johansson?" she asked. (The lab doesn't seem the same without his long glum face—or without Pete.)

(He's gone to help out in) "Africa, I think." (A colossal job before us, too big, too sudden.)

(Too cruel!)

Nodding: (Yes.) Eyes to Manzelli: (Question.)

Manzelli's gaze rested on Sheila with a probing intensity. She shivered, and Grunewald gave his partner a reproachful look.

(I came up) "From Long Island today." Bitterness in her smile, she has grown harder, and a nod: (Yes, they seem to think it's all right to let me loose now. At least, they had no way to compel me, and too much else to do to worry about me in any case.)

A grayness flitted through Grunewald's expression. (You came up to say good-by, didn't you?)

129

(I wanted to) "See" (the) "place" (once again, only for a little while. It holds so many of his days).

Sudden pleading in her: "He is dead, isn't he?"

Shrug, pity: (We can't say. But the ship is months overdue, and only a major disaster could have stopped her. She may have run into the) "Inhibitor field" (out in space, in spite of all precautions).

Sheila walked slowly past him. She went over to Pete's desk and stroked her fingers across the back of his chair.

Grunewald cleared his throat. (Are you) "Leaving civilization?"

She nodded mutely. *It is too big for me, too cold and strange.*

(There is still) "Work to do," he said.

She shook her head. (Not for me. It is not a work I want or understand.) Taking up the cigarette lighter, she dropped it into her purse, smiling a little.

Grunewald and Manzelli traded another look. This time Manzelli made a sign of agreement.

(We have been) "Doing work" (here which might— interest you), said Grunewald. *Give you hope. Give you back your tomorrows.*

The brown eyes that turned to him were almost unfocused. He thought that her face was like white paper, stretched across the bones; and some Chinese artist had penned the delicate blue tracery of veins across her temples and hands.

He tried awkwardly to explain. The nature of the inhibitor field had been more fully worked out since the star ship left. Even before that time, it had been possible to generate the field artificially and study its effects; now Grunewald and Manzelli had gotten together on a project of creating the same thing on a huge scale. It shouldn't take much apparatus—a few tons, perhaps; and once the field was set up, using a nuclear disintegrator to furnish the necessary power, solar energy should be enough to maintain it.

The project was highly unofficial: now that the first press of necessity was gone, those scientists who chose were free to work on whatever suited their own fancy, and materials weren't difficult to obtain. There was a small organization which helped get what was necessary; all that Grunewald and Manzelli were doing here at the Institute was testing, the actual construction went on elsewhere. Their labor seemed harmless to everyone else, a little dull compared to what was going on in other lines of endeavor. No one paid any attention to it, or reasoned below the surface of Grunewald's public explanation.

Sheila regarded him vaguely, and he wondered about the regions into which her inner self had gone. "Why?" she asked. "What is it you're really doing?"

Manzelli smiled, with a harshness over him. (Isn't it obvious? We mean to) "Build an orbital space station" (and set it going several thousand miles above the surface). "Full-scale field generators" (in it. We'll bring mankind back to the) "Old days."

She didn't cry out, or gasp, or even laugh. She only nodded, as if it were a blurred image of no meaning.

(Retreat from reality—how sane are you?) asked Grunewald's eyes.

(What reality?) she flashed at him.

Manzelli shrugged. He knew she wouldn't tell anyone, he could read that much in her, and that was what counted. If it didn't give her the excited joy Grunewald had hoped for, it was no concern of his.

Sheila wandered over to one side of the room. A collection of apparatus there looked peculiarly medical. She saw the table with its straps, the drawer with hypodermic needles and ampules, the machine which crouched blackly near the head of the table—— "What is this?" she asked. Her tone should have told them that she knew already, but they were too immersed in their own wishes.

"Modified electric-shock treatment," said Grunewald. He explained that in the first weeks of the change there had been an attempt to study the functional aspects of intelligence by systematic destruction of the cerebral cortex cells in animals, and measurement of the effects. But it had soon been abandoned as too inhumane and relatively useless. "I thought you knew" (about it), he finished. (It was) "In the biology and psych departments when Pete" (was still here. I remember he) "protested strongly" (against it. Didn't he gripe to) "you" (about it too)?

131

Sheila nodded dimly.

"The change" (made) "men cruel," said Manzelli. (And) "Now" (they) "aren't" (even that, any longer. They've become something other than man, and this world of rootless intellect has lost all its old dreams and loves. We want to restore humanness).

Sheila turned away from the ugly black machine. "Good-by," she said.

"I—well——" Grunewald looked at the floor. "Keep in touch, won't you?" (Let us know where you are, so if Pete comes back——)

Her smile was as remote as death. (He will never come back. But good-by, now.)

She went out the door and down the corridor. Near the staircase was a washroom door. It was not marked "Men" or "Women," even the Western world had gone beyond such prudery, and she went in and looked in a mirror. The face that regarded her was hollow, and the hair hung lank and dull to her shoulders. She made an effort with comb and water to spruce up, not knowing or caring why she did, and then went down the stairway to the first floor.

The door to the director's office stood open, letting a breeze find its way between the windows and the building entrance. There were quiet machines inside, probably doing the work of a large secretarial staff. Sheila went past the outer suite and knocked on the open door of the inner office.

Helga Arnulfsen glanced up from her desk. She'd grown a little thin too, Sheila realized, and there was a darkness in her eyes. But even if she was more informally dressed than had once been her habit, she was strong and smooth to look on. Her voice, which had always been husky, lifted a trifle in surprise: "Sheila!"

"How do you do?"

"Come in," (do come in, sit down. It's been a long time since I saw you). Helga was smiling as she came around the desk and took Sheila's hand, but her fingers were cold.

She pressed a button and the door closed. (Now we can have) "Privacy," she said. (This is the sign I'm not to be bothered.) She pulled up a chair across from Sheila's and sat down, crossing her long trim legs man-fashion. "Well, good" (to see you. I hope you're feeling well.) *You don't look well, poor kid.*

"I——" Sheila clasped her hands and unclasped them again and picked at the purse in her lap. "I——" (Why did I come?)

Eyes: (Because of Pete.)

Nod: (Yes. Yes, that must be it. Sometimes I don't know why—— But we both loved him, didn't we?)

"You," said Helga without tone, "are the only one he cared for." *And you hurt him. Your suffering was grief within him.*

I know. That's the worst of it. (And still) "He wasn't the same man," said Sheila. (He changed too much, like all the world. Even as I held him, he slipped by me, time itself carried him away.) "I lost him even before he died."

"No. You had him, it was always you." Helga shrugged. "Well, life goes on," (in an amputated fashion. We eat and breathe and sleep and work, because there is nothing else we can do.)

"You have strength," said Sheila. (You have endured where I couldn't.)

"Oh, I kept going," answered Helga.

"You still have tomorrow."

"Yes, I suppose so."

Sheila smiled, it trembled on her mouth. (I'm luckier than you are. I have yesterday.)

"They may come back," said Helga. (There's no telling what has happened to them. Have you the courage to wait?)

"No," said Sheila. "Their bodies may come back," (but not Pete. He has changed too much, and I can't change with him. Nor would I want to be a weight around his neck.)

Helga laid a hand on Sheila's arm. How thin it was! You could feel the bones underneath. "Wait," she said. "Therapy" (is progressing. You can be brought up to) "Normal" (in—well—a) "few years, at most."

"I don't think so."

There was a touch of contempt, thinly veiled, in the cool blue eyes. *Do you want to live up to the future? Down underneath, do you really desire to keep pace?* "What else" (can you do) "but wait? Unless suicide——"

"No, not that either." (There are still mountains, deep valleys, shining rivers, sun and moon and the high stars of winter.) "I'll find my—adjustment."

(I've kept in touch with) "Kearnes." (He) "Seemed (to) "think" (you were) "progressing."

"Oh, yes." *I've learned to hide it. There are too many eyes in this new world.* "But I didn't come to talk about myself, Helga." (I just came to say) "Good-by."

"Where" (are you going? I have to keep in touch with you, if he should come back.)

"I'll write" (and let you know).

"Or give a message to a Sensitive." (The postal system is obsolete.)

That too? I remember old Mr. Barneveldt, shuffling down the street in his blue uniform, when I was a little girl. He used to have a piece of candy for me.

"Look, I'm getting hungry," said Helga. (Why don't we go have) "Lunch?"

(No, thank you. I don't feel like it.) Sheila got up. "Good-by, Helga."

"Not good-by, Sheila. We'll see you again, and you'll be well then."

"Yes," said Sheila. "I'll be all right. But good-by."

She walked out of the office and the building. There were more people abroad now, and she mingled with them. A doorway across the street offered a hidden place.

She felt no sense of farewell. There was an emptiness in her, as if grief and loneliness and bewilderment had devoured themselves. Now and then one of the shadows flitted across her mind, but they weren't frightening any longer. Almost, she pitied them. Poor ghosts! They would die soon.

She saw Helga emerge and walk alone down the street, toward some place where she would swallow a solitary lunch before going back to work. Sheila smiled, shaking her head a little. *Poor efficient Helga!*

Presently Grunewald and Manzelli came out and went the same way, lost in conversation. Sheila's heart gave a small leap. The palms of her hands were cold and wet.

She waited till the men were out of sight, then crossed the street again and re-entered the Institute.

The noise of her shoes was hard on the stairway. She breathed deeply, trying for steadiness. When she came out on the seventh floor, she stood for a minute waiting for the self-control she needed. Then she ran down the hall to the physical laboratory.

The door gaped ajar. She hesitated again, looking at the unfinished machine within. Hadn't Grunewald told her about some fantastic scheme to——? No matter. It couldn't work. He and Manzelli, that whole little band of recidivists, were insane.

Am I insane? she wondered. If so, there was an odd strength in her. She needed more resolution for what she was going to do than it took to put a gun barrel in her mouth and squeeze a trigger.

The shock machine lay like some armored animal beside the table. She worked swiftly, adjusting it. Memory of Pete's anger at its early use had, indeed, come back to her in the house of isolation; and Kearnes had been pleased to give her all the texts she asked for, glad that she was finding an objective interest. She smiled again. Poor Kearnes! How she had fooled him.

The machine hummed, warming up. She took a small bundle from her purse and unwrapped it. Syringe, needle, bottle of anesthetic, electrode paste, cord to tie to the switch so she could pull it with her teeth. And a timer for the switch, too. She had to estimate the safe time for what was necessary, she would be unconscious when the process must be stopped.

Maybe it wouldn't work. Quite likely her brain would simply fry in her skull. What of it?

She smiled out the window as she injected herself. Good-by, sun, good-by, blue heaven, clouds, rain, airy song of home-bound birds. Good-by and thank you.

Stripping off her clothes, she lay on the table and fastened the electrodes in place. They felt cold against her skin. Some of the straps were easy to buckle, but the right arm—well, she had come prepared, she had a long belt that went under the table, around her wrist, a padlock she could snap shut. Now she was immobile.

135

Her eyes darkened as the drug took hold. It was good to sleep.

Now—one quick jerk with her teeth.

THUNDER AND FIRE AND SHATTERING DARK-NESS

RUIN AND HORROR AND LIGHTNING

PAIN PAIN PAIN

CHAPTER *19*

"HELLO, Earth. Peter Corinth calling Earth from Star Ship I, homeward bound."

Buzz and murmur of cosmic interference, the talking of the stars. Earth a swelling blue brilliance against night, her moon like a pearl hung on the galaxy's breast, the sun wreathed in flame.

"Hello, Earth. Come in, come in. Can you hear me, Earth?"

Click, click, zzzzz, mmmmmm, voices across the sky. *Hello, Sheila!*

The planet grew before them. The ship's drive purred and rumbled, every plate in the hull trembled with thrusting energies, there was a wild fine singing in the crystals of the metal. Corinth realized that he was shaking too, but he didn't want to control himself, not now.

"Hello, Earth," he said monotonously into the radio. They were moving well under the speed of light and their signal probed blindly ahead of them, through the dark. "Hello, Earth, can you hear me? This is Star Ship I, calling from space, homeward bound."

Lewis growled something which meant: (Maybe they've given up radio since we left. All these months——"

Corinth shook his head: "They'd still have monitors of some kind, I'm sure." To the microphone: "Hello, Earth, come in, Earth. Anyone on Earth hear me?"

"If some ham—a five-year-old kid, I bet, in Russia or India or Africa—picks it up, he'll have to get the word to a transmitter which can reach us," said Lewis. "It takes time. Just relax, Pete."

"A matter of time!" Corinth turned from the seat. "You're right, I suppose. We'll make planetfall in hours, anyway. But I did want to have a real welcome prepared for us!"

"A dozen Limfjord oysters on the half shell, with lots of lemon juice," said Lewis dreamily, speaking all the words aloud. "Rhine wine, of course—say a '37. Baby shrimp in fresh mayonnaise, on French bread with fresh-churned butter. Smoked eel with cold scrambled eggs on pumpernickel, don't forget the chives——"

Corinth grinned, though half his mind was lost with Sheila, off alone with her in some place of sunlight. It was good, it felt strangely warm, to sit and exchange common-places, even if those were overtly little more than a word and a shift of expression. All the long way home, they had argued like drunken gods, exploring their own intellects; but it had been a means of shutting out the stupendous dark quiet. Now they were back to man's hearth fire.

"Hello, Star Ship I."

They jerked wildly about to face the receiver. The voice that came was faint, blurred with the noise of sun and stars, but it was human. It was home.

"Why," whispered Lewis in awe, "why, he's even got a Brooklyn accent."

"Hello, Star Ship I. This is New York calling you. Can you hear me?"

"Yes," said Corinth, his throat dry, and waited for the signal to leap across millions of miles.

"Had a devil of a time getting you," said the voice conversationally, after the time lag had gone by in whining, crackling blankness. "Had to allow for Doppler effect—you must be coming in like a bat out of Chicago, are your pants on fire or something?" He mentioned nothing of the engineering genius which had made communication possible at all; it was a minor job now. "Congratulations, though! All okay?"

"Fine," said Lewis. "Had some trouble, but we're com-

ing home in one piece and expect to be greeted properly."
He hesitated for a moment. "How's Earth?"

"Good enough. Though I'll bet you won't recognize the
place. Things are changing so fast it's a real relief to talk
good old United States once again. Prolly the last time I'll
ever do it. What the devil happened to you, anyway?"

"We'll explain later," said Corinth shortly. "How are
our—associates?"

"Okay, I guess. I'm just a technician at Brookhaven, you
know, I'm not acquainted. But I'll pass the word along.
You'll land here, I suppose?"

"Yes, in about——" Corinth made a swift estimate involving the simultaneous solution of a number of differential equations. "Six hours."

"Okay, we'll——" The tone faded away. They caught
one more word, "——band——" and then there was only
the stillness.

"Hello, New York, you've lost the beam," said Corinth.

"Ah, forget it," said Lewis. "Turn it off, why don't
you?"

"But——"

"We've waited so long that we can wait six hours more.
Isn't worthwhile tinkering around that way."

"Ummmm—well——" Corinth yielded. "Hello, New
York. Hello, Earth. This is Star Ship I signing off. Over
and out."

"I did want to talk to Sheila," he added.

"You'll have plenty of time for that, laddy," answered
Lewis. "I think right now we ought to be taking a few
more observations on the drive. It's got a fluttery note that
might mean something. Nobody's ever operated one continuously as long as we have, and there may be cumulative
effects——"

"Crystal fatigue, perhaps," said Corinth. "Okay, you
win." He gave himself to his instruments.

Earth grew before them. They, who had crossed light-
years in hours, had to limp home now at mere hundreds
of miles a second; even their new reactions weren't fast
enough to handle translight speeds this near a planet. But
theirs would probably be the last ship so limited, thought
Corinth. At the fantastic rate of post-change technological

advance, the next vessel should be a dream of perfection: as if the Wright brothers had built a transatlantic clipper for their second working model. He imagined that his own lifetime would see engineering carried to some kind of ultimate, reaching the bounds imposed by natural law. Thereafter man would have to find a new field of intellectual adventure, and he thought he knew what it would be. He looked at the swelling lovely planet with a kind of tenderness. *Ave atque vale!*

The crescent became a ragged, cloudy disc as they swung around toward the day side. Then, subtly, it was no longer before them but below them, and they heard the first thin shriek of cloven air. They swept over a vastness of moonlit Pacific, braking, and saw dawn above the Sierra Nevada. America fell beneath them, huge and green and beautiful, a strong-ribbed land, and the Mississippi was a silver thread across her. Then they slanted down, and the spires of Manhattan rose against the sea.

Corinth's heart slammed in the cage of his breast. *Be still,* he told it, *be still and wait. There is time now.* He guided the ship toward Brookhaven, where the spacefield was a slash of gray, and saw another bright spear cradled there. So they had already begun on the next ship.

There was a tiny shock as the hull found its berth. Lewis reached over to cut off the engines. When they died, Corinth's ears rang with the sudden quiet. He had not realized how much a part of him that ceaseless drumming was.

"Come on!" He was out of his seat and across the narrow cabin before Lewis had stirred. His fingers trembled as they wove across the intricate pattern of the electronic lock. The inner door swung smoothly open, and then the outer door was open too, and he caught a breath of salt air, blown in from the sea.

Sheila! Where is Sheila? He tumbled down the ladder in the cradle, his form dark against the metal of the hull. It was pocked and blistered, that metal, streaked with curious crystallization-patterns; the ship had traveled far and strangely. When he hit the ground he overbalanced, falling, but he was up again before anyone could help him.

"Sheila." he cried.

Felix Mandelbaum stepped forth, holding out his hands.

139

He looked very old and tired, burned out by strain. He took Corinth's hands in his own but did not speak.

"Where's Sheila?" whispered Corinth. "Where is she?"

Mandelbaum shook his head. Lewis was climbing down now, more cautiously. Rossman went to meet him, looking away from Corinth. The others followed—they were all Brookhaven people, no close friends, but they looked away.

Corinth tried to swallow and couldn't. "Dead?" he asked. The wind murmured around him, ruffling his hair.

"No," said Mandelbaum. "Nor is she mad. But——" He shook his head, and the beaked face wrinkled up. "No."

Corinth drew a breath that shuddered in his lungs. Looking at him, they saw the blankness of will descend. He would not let himself weep.

"Go ahead," he said. "Tell me."

"It was about six weeks ago," Mandelbaum said. "She couldn't stand any more, I guess. She got hold of an electric-shock machine."

Corinth nodded, very slowly. "And destroyed her brain," he finished.

"No. Not that, though it was touch and go for a while." Mandelbaum took the physicist's arm. "Let's put it this way: she is the old Sheila, like before the change. Almost."

Corinth was dimly aware how fresh and live the sea wind felt in his nostrils.

"Come along, Pete," said Mandelbaum. "I'll take you to her."

Corinth followed him off the field.

The psychiatrist Kearnes met them at Bellevue. His face was like wood, but there was no feeling of shame in him and none of blame in Corinth. The man had done his best, with the inadequate knowledge at his disposal, and failed; that was a fact of reality, nothing more.

"She fooled me," he said. "I thought she was straightening out. I didn't realize how much control even an insane person would have with the changed nervous system. Nor, I suppose, did I realize how hard it was for her all along. None of us who endured the change will ever know what

140

a nightmare it must have been for those who couldn't adapt."

Dark wings beating, and Sheila alone. Nightfall, and Sheila alone.

"She was quite insane when she did it?" asked Corinth. His voice was flat.

"What is sanity? Perhaps she did the wisest thing. Was the eventual prospect of being cured, when we learn how, worth that kind of existence?"

"What were the effects?"

"Well, it was a clumsy job, of course. Several bones were broken in the convulsions, and she'd have died if she hadn't been found in time." Kearnes laid a hand on Corinth's shoulder. "The actual volume of destroyed cerebral tissue was small, but of course it was in the most critical area of the brain."

"Felix told me she's—making a good recovery."

"Oh, yes." Kearnes smiled wryly, as if he had a sour taste in his mouth. "It isn't hard for us to understand pre-change human psychology—now. I used the triple-pronged approach developed by Gravenstein and de la Garde since the change. Symbological re-evaluation, cybernetic neurology, and somatic co-ordination treatments. There was enough sound tissue to take over the functions of the damaged part, with proper guidance, once the psychosis had been lifted. I think she can be discharged from here in about three months."

He drew a deep breath. "She will be a normal, healthy pre-change human with an I.Q. of about 150."

"I see——" Corinth nodded. "Well—what are the chances of restoring her?"

"It will take years, at best, before we're able to recreate nervous tissue. It doesn't regenerate, you know, even with artificial stimulation. We'll have to create life itself synthetically, and telescope a billion years of evolution to develop the human brain cell, and duplicate the precise gene pattern of the patient, and even then—I wonder."

"I see."

"You can visit her for a short while. We have told her you were alive."

"What did she do?"

"Cried a good deal, of course. That's a healthy symptom. You can stay about half an hour if you don't excite her too much." Kearnes gave him the room number and went back into his office.

Corinth took the elevator and walked down a long quiet hallway that smelled of rain-wet roses. When he came to Sheila's room, the door stood ajar and he hesitated a little, glancing in. It was like a forest bower, ferns and trees and the faint twitter of nesting birds; a waterfall was running somewhere, and the air had the tingle of earth and greenness. Mostly illusion, he supposed, but if it gave her comfort——

He went in, over to the bed which rested beneath a sun-dappled willow. "Hello, darling," he said.

The strangest thing was that she hadn't changed. She looked as she had when they were first married, young and fair, her hair curled softly about a face which was still a little pale, her eyes full of luster as they turned to him. The white nightgown, a fluffy thing from her own wardrobe, made her seem only half grown.

"Pete," she said.

He stooped over and kissed her, very gently. Her response was somehow remote, almost like a stranger's. As her hands caressed his face, he noticed that the wedding ring was gone.

"You lived." She spoke it with a kind of wonder. "You came back."

"To you, Sheila," he said, and sat down beside her.

She shook her head. "No," she answered.

"I love you," he said in his helplessness.

"I loved you too." Her voice was still quiet, far away, and he saw the dreaminess in her eyes. "That's why I did this."

He sat holding himself in, fighting for calm. There were thunders in his head.

"I don't remember you too well, you know," she said. "I suppose my memory was damaged a little. It all seems many years ago, and you like a dream I loved." She smiled. "How thin you are, Pete! And hard, somehow. Everybody has grown so hard."

"No," he said. "They all care for you."

142

"It isn't the old kind of caring. Not the kind I knew. And you aren't Pete anymore." She sat up, her voice rising a little. "Pete died in the change. I watched him die. You're a nice man, and it hurts me to look at you, but you aren't Pete."

"Take it easy, darling," he said.

"I couldn't go ahead with you," she said, "and I wouldn't give you—or myself—that kind of burden. Now I've gone back. And you don't know how wonderful it is. Lonely but wonderful. There's peace in it."

"I still want you," he said.

"No. Don't lie to me. Don't you see, it isn't necessary." Sheila smiled across a thousand years. "You can sit there like that, your face all frozen—why, you aren't Pete. But I wish you well."

He knew then what she needed, and let himself go, surrendering will and understanding. He knelt by her bed and wept, and she comforted him as well as she could.

CHAPTER 20

THERE is an island in mid-Pacific, not far off the equator, which lies distant from the world of man. The old shipping routes and the later transoceanic airlines followed tracks beyond its horizon, and the atoll had been left to sun and wind and the crying of gulls.

For a brief while it had known humankind. The slow blind patience of coral polyps had built it up, and days and nights had ground its harsh wet face into soil, and the seeds of plants had been blown on a long journey to find it. A few coconuts washed up in the surf, and presently there were trees. They stood for hundreds of years, perhaps, until a canoe came over the world's rim.

Those were Polynesians, tall brown men whose race had wandered far in the search for Hawaiki the beautiful.

There was sun and salt on them, and they thought little of crossing a thousand miles of emptiness, for they had the stars and the great sea currents to guide them and their own arms to paddle, *tohiha, hioha, itoki, itoki!* When they drew their boat ashore and had made sacrifice to shark-toothed Nan, they wound hibiscus blooms in their long hair and danced on the beach; for they had looked on the island and found it good.

Then they went away, but the next year—or the year after that, or the year after that, for the ocean was big and time was forever—they came back with others, bringing pigs and women, and that night fires burned tall on the beach. Afterward a village of thatch huts arose, and naked brown children tumbled in the surf, and fishermen went beyond the lagoon with much laughter. And this lasted for a hundred years, or two hundred, before the pale men came.

Their big white-winged canoes stopped only a few times at this island, which was not an important one, but nonetheless faithfully discharged their usual cargo of smallpox, measles, and tuberculosis, so that there were not many of the brown folk left. Afterward some resistance was built up, aided by Caucasian blood, and it was time for copra planters, religion, Mother Hubbards, and international conferences to determine whether this atoll, among others, belonged to London, Paris, Berlin, or Washington—large villages on the other side of the world.

A *modus vivendi* was finally reached, involving copra, Christianity, tobacco, and trading schooners. The island people, by this time a mixture of several races, were reasonably satisfied, though they did have many toothaches; and when one of their young men, who through a long chain of circumstances had studied in America, came back and sighed for the old days, the people laughed at him. They had only vague memories of that time, handed down through a series of interested missionaries.

Then someone in an office on the other side of the world decided that an island was needed. It may have been for a naval base, or perhaps an experimental station—the pale men had so many wars, and spent the rest of their time preparing for them. It does not matter any longer why the

144

atoll was desired, for there are no men on it now and the gulls don't care. The natives were moved elsewhere, and spent some quiet years in a sick longing for home. Nobody paid any attention to this, for the island was needed to safeguard the freedom of man, and after a time the older generation died off and the younger generation forgot. Meanwhile the white men disturbed the gulls for a little, putting up buildings and filling the lagoon with ships.

Then, for some unimportant reason, the island was abandoned. It may have been through treaty, possibly through a defeat in war or an economic collapse. The wind and rain and creeping vines had never been defeated, only contained. Now they began the task of demolition.

For a few centuries, men had disturbed the timelessness of days and nights, rain and sun and stars and hurricanes, but now they were gone again. The surf rolled and chewed at the reef, the slow chill sliding of underwater currents gnawed at the foundations, but there were many polyps and they were still building. The island would endure for a goodly fraction of a million years, so there was no hurry about anything. By day fish leaped in the waters, and gulls hovered overhead, and the trees and bamboo grew with frantic haste; at night the moon was cold on tumbling surf and a phosphorescent track swirled behind the great shark who patrolled the outer waters. And there was peace.

The airjet whispered down out of darkness and the high bright stars. Invisible fingers of radar probed earthward, and a voice muttered over a beam. "Down—this way—okay, easy does it." The jet bounced to a halt in a clearing, and two men came out.

They were met by others, indistinct shadows in the moon-spattered night. One of them spoke with a dry Australian twang: "Dr. Grunewald, Dr. Manzelli, may I present Major Rosovsky—Sri Ramavashtar—Mr. Hwang Pu-Yi——" He went on down the list; there were about a score present, including the two Americans.

Not so long ago, it would have been a strange, even impossible group: a Russian officer, a Hindu mystic, a French philosopher and religious writer, an Irish politician, a Chinese commissar, an Australian engineer, a Swedish
145

financier—it was as if all the earth had gathered for a quiet insurrection. But none of them were now what they had been, and the common denominator was a yearning for something lost.

"I've brought the control apparatus," said Grunewald briskly. "How about the heavy stuff?"

"It's all here. We can start anytime," said the Irishman.

Grunewald glanced at his watch. "It's a couple of hours to midnight," he said aloud. "Can we be ready by then?"

"I think so," said the Russian. "It is almost all assembled."

Walking down toward the beach, he gestured at the bulking shape which lay black and awkward on the moon-whitened lagoon. He and one comrade had gotten the tramp steamer months ago and outfitted her with machines such that they two could sail her around the world. That had been their part of the job: not too difficult for determined men in the confusion of a dying civilization. They had sailed through the Baltic, picking up some of their cargo in Sweden, and had also touched in France, Italy, Egypt, and India on their way to the agreed destination. For some days, now, the work of assembling the spaceship and her load had progressed rapidly.

The surf roared and rumbled, a deep full noise that shivered underfoot, and spouted whitely toward the constellations. Sand and coral scrunched beneath boots, the palms and bamboos rustled dryly with the small wind, and a disturbed parakeet racketed in the dark. Beyond this little beating of sound, there were only silence and sleep.

Further on, the ruin of an old barracks moldered in its shroud of vines. Grunewald smelled the flowers there, and the heavy dampness of rotting wood—it was a pungency which made his head swim. On the other side of the ruin stood some tents, recently put up, and above them towered the spaceship.

That was a clean and beautiful thing, like a pillar of gray ice under the moon, poised starward. Grunewald looked at her with a curious blend of feelings: taut fierce glory of conquest, heart-catching knowledge of her loveliness, wistfulness that soon he would not understand the transcendent logic which had made her swift designing and building possible.

He looked at Manzelli. "I envy you, my friend," he said simply.

Several men were to ride her up, jockey her into an orbit, and do the final work of assembling and starting the field generator she bore. Then they would die, for there had not been time to prepare a means for their return.

Grunewald felt time like a hound on his heels. Soon the next star ship would be ready, and they were building others everywhere. Then there would be no stopping the march of the race, and of time. Tonight the last hope of mankind—human mankind—was being readied; there could not be another, if this failed.

"I think," he said, "that all the world will cry with relief before sunrise."

"No," said the Australian practically. "They'll be madder'n a nest of hornets. You'll have to allow a while for them to realize they've been saved."

Well, there would be time, then. The spaceship was equipped with defenses beyond the capacity of pre-change man to overcome in less than a century. Her robots would destroy any other ships or missiles sent up from Earth. And man, the whole living race, would have a chance to catch his breath and remember his first loves, and after that he would not want to attack the spaceship.

The others had unloaded the jet from America and brought its delicate cargo to this place. Now they laid the crates on the ground, and Grunewald and Manzelli began opening them with care. Someone switched on a floodlight, and in its harsh white glare they forgot the moon and the sea around them.

Nor were they aware of the long noiseless form which slipped overhead and hung there like a shark swimming in the sky, watching. Only after it had spoken to them did they look up.

The amplified voice had been gentle, there was almost a note of regret in it. "Sorry to disappoint you, but you've done enough."

Staring wildly upward, Grunewald saw the steel shimmer above and his heart stumbled within him. The Russian

147

yanked out a pistol and fired, the shots yammering futilely under the steady beat of surf. A gabble came from wakened birds, and their wings flapped loud among the soughing palms.

Manzelli cursed, whirled on his heel, and plunged into the spaceship. There were guns in it which could bring down that riding menace, and—Grunewald, diving for cover, saw a turret in the vessel's flank swing about and thrust a nose skyward. He threw himself on his belly. That cannon fired atomic shells!

From the hovering enemy sprang a beam of intense, eye-searing flame. The cannon muzzle slumped, glowed white. The thin finger wrote destruction down the flank of the ship until it reached the cones of her gravitic drive. There it played for minutes, and the heat of melting steel prickled men's faces.

A giant atomic-hydrogen torch—Grunewald's mind was dazed. *We can't take off now——*

Slowly, the very walls of the crippled spaceship began to glow red. The Swede screamed and pulled a ring off his finger. Manzelli stumbled out of the ship, crying. The force-field died, the machines began to cool again, but there was something broken in the men who stood waiting. Only the heavy sobs of Manzelli spoke.

The enemy craft—it was a star ship, they saw now—remained where it was, but a small antigravity raft floated out of her belly and drifted earthward. There were men standing on it, and one woman. None of the cabal moved as the raft grounded.

Grunewald took one step forward then, and stopped with his shoulders slumping. "Felix," he said in a dead voice. "Pete. Helga."

Mandelbaum nodded. The single floodlight threw a hard black shadow across his face. He waited on the raft while three quiet burly men, who had been detectives in the old world, went among the conspirators and collected the guns they had thrown away as too hot to hold. Then he joined the police on the ground. Corinth and Helga followed.

"Surely you didn't expect to get away with this," said Mandelbaum. His voice was not exultant but tired. He shook his head. "Why, the Observers had your pitiful little scheme watched almost from its beginning. Your very secrecy gave you away."

"Then why did you let it get so far?" asked the Australian. His tones were thick with anger.

"Partly to keep you out of worse mischief and partly so you'd draw in others of like mind and thus locate them for us," said Mandelbaum. "We waited till we knew you were all set to go, and then we came."

"That was vicious," said the Frenchman. "It was the sort of coldbloodedness that has grown up since the change. I suppose the intelligent, the expedient thing for you now is to shoot us down."

"Why, no," said Mandelbaum mildly. "As a matter of fact, we used a reaction damper along with the metal-heating field, just to keep your cartridges from going off and hurting you. After all, we'll have to find out from you who else has backed you. And then you all have good minds, lots of energy and courage—quite a big potential value. It's not your fault the change drove you insane."

"Insane!" The Russian spat, and recovered himself with a shaking effort. "Insane you call us!"

"Well," said Mandelbaum, "if the delusion that you few have the right to make decisions for all the race, and force them through, isn't megalomania, then what is? If you really had a case, you could have presented it to the world soon enough."

"The world has been blinded," said the Hindu with dignity. "It can no longer see the truth. I myself have lost the feeble glimpse of the ultimate I once had, though at least I know it was lost."

"What you mean," said Mandelbaum coldly, "is that your mind's become too strong for you to go into the kind of trance which was your particular fetalization, but you still feel the need for it."

The Hindu shrugged contemptuously.

Grunewald looked at Corinth. "I thought you were my friend, Pete," he whispered. "And after what the change did to your wife, I thought you could see——"

"He's had nothing to do with this," said Helga, stepping forward a little and taking Corinth's arm. "I'm the one who fingered you, Grunewald. Pete just came along with us
149

tonight as a physicist, to look over your apparatus and salvage it for something useful." *Occupational therapy—O Pete, Pete, you have been hurt so much!*

Corinth shook his head and spoke harshly, with an anger new to his mildness. "Never mind finding excuses for me. I'd have done this alone, if I'd known what you planned. Because what would Sheila be like if the old world came back?"

"You'll be cured," said Mandelbaum. "Your cases aren't violent, I think the new psychiatric techniques can straighten you out pretty quick."

"I wish you'd kill me instead," said the Australian.

Manzelli was still crying. The sobs tore at him like claws.

"Why can you not see?" asked the Frenchman. "Are all the glories man has won in the past to go for nothing? Before he has even found God, will you turn God into a nursery tale? What have you given him in return for the splendors of his art, the creation in his hands, and the warm little pleasures when his day's work is done? You have turned him into a calculating machine, and the body and the soul can wither amidst his new equations."

Mandelbaum shrugged. "The change wasn't my idea," he said. "If you believe in God, then this looks rather like His handiwork, His way of taking the next step forward."

"It is forward from the intellectual's point of view," said the Frenchman. "To a nearsighted, soft-bellied, flatulent professor, this is no doubt progress."

"Do I look like a professor?" grunted Mandelbaum. "I was riveting steel when you were reading your first books about the beauties of nature. I was having my face kicked in by company goons when you were writing about the sin of pride and battle. You loved the working man, but you wouldn't invite him to your table, now would you? When little Jean-Pierre, he was a divinity student before the war, when he was caught spying for our side, he held out for twenty-four hours against everything the Germans could do to him and gave the rest of us a chance to escape. Meanwhile, as I recall, you were safe in the States writing propaganda. Judas priest, why don't you ever try those things you're so ready to theorize about?"

The dragging weariness lifted from him as he swung

into the old joy of struggle. His voice raised itself in a hard fierce tone, like hammers on iron. "The trouble with all of you is that one way or another, you're all afraid to face life. Instead of trying to shape the future, you've been wanting a past which is already a million years behind us. You've lost your old illusions and you haven't got what it takes to make new and better ones for yourselves."

"Including the American delusion of 'Progress,'" snapped the Chinese.

"Who said anything about that? That's forgotten too, obsolete junk—another shibboleth born of stupidity and greed and smugness. Sure, all our past has been stripped from us. Sure, it's a terrible feeling, bare and lonely like this. But do you think man can't strike a new balance? Do you think we can't build a new culture, with its own beauty and delight and dreams, now that we've broken out of the old cocoon? And do you think that men—men with strength and hope in them, all races, all over the world—want to go back? I tell you they don't. The very fact you tried this secretly shows you knew the same thing.

"What did the old world offer to ninety per cent of the human race? Toil, ignorance, disease, war, oppression, want, fear, from the filthy birth to the miserable grave. If you were born into a lucky land, you might fill your belly and have a few shiny toys to play with, but there was no hope in you, no vision, no purpose. The fact that one civilization after another went down into ruin shows we weren't fitted for it; we were savages by nature. Now we have a chance to get off that wheel of history and go somewhere—nobody knows where, nobody can even guess, but our eyes have been opened and you wanted to close them again!"

Mandelbaum broke off, sighed, and turned to his detectives. "Take 'em away, boys," he said.

The cabal were urged onto the raft—gently, there was no need for roughness and no malice. Mandelbaum stood watching as the raft lifted slowly up into the star ship. Then he turned to the long metal form on the ground.

"What a heroic thing!" he muttered, shaking his head. "Futile, but heroic. Those are good men. I hope it won't take too long to salvage them."

Corinth's grin was crooked. "Of course, *we* are absolutely right," he said.

Mandelbaum chuckled. "Sorry for the lecture," he replied. "Old habit too strong—a fact has to have a moral tag on it—well, we, the human race, ought to get over that pretty soon."

The physicist sobered. "You have to have some kind of morality," he said.

"Sure. Like you have to have motives for doing anything at all. Still, I think we're beyond that smug sort of code which proclaimed crusades and burned heretics and threw dissenters into concentration camps. We need more personal and less public honor."

Mandelbaum yawned then, stretching his wiry frame till it seemed the bones must crack. "Long ride, and not even a proper gun battle at the end," he said. The raft was coming down again, automatically. "I'm for some sleep. We can look over this mess of junk in the morning. Coming?"

"Not just yet," said Corinth. "I'm too tired." (I want to think.) "I'll walk over toward the beach."

"Okay." Mandelbaum smiled, with a curious tenderness on his lips. "Good night."

"Good night." Corinth turned and walked from the clearing. Helga went wordlessly beside him.

They came out of the jungle and stood on sands that were like frost under the moon. Beyond the reef, the surf flamed and crashed, and the ocean was roiled and streaked with the cold flimmer of phosphorescence. The big stars were immensely high overhead, but the night sky was like crystal. Corinth felt the sea wind in his face, sharp and salt, damp with the thousand watery miles it had swept across. Behind him, the jungle rustled and whispered to itself, and the sand gritted tinily underfoot. He was aware of it all with an unnatural clarity, as if he had been drained of everything that was himself and was now only a vessel of images.

He looked at Helga, where she stood holding his arm. Her face was sharply outlined against the further darkness, and her hair—she had unbound it—fluttered loosely in the wind, white in the pouring unreal moonlight. Their two shadows were joined into one, long and blue across the glittering sand. He could feel the rhythm of her breathing where she stood against him.

They had no need to speak. Too much understanding had grown up between them, they had shared too much of work and watching, and now they stood for a while in silence. The sea talked to them, giant pulsing of waves, boom where they hit the reef, rush where they streamed back into the water. The wind hissed and murmured under the sky.

Gravitation (sun, moon, stars, the tremendous unity which is space-time)

$+$ Coriolis force (the planet turning, turning, on its way through miles and years)

$+$ Fluid friction (the oceans grinding, swirling, roaring between narrow straits, spuming and thundering over rock)

$+$ Temperature differential (sunlight like warm rain, ice and darkness, clouds, mists, wind and storm)

$+$ Vulcanism (fire deep in the belly of the planet, sliding of unimaginable rock masses, smoke and lava, the raising of new mountains with snow on their shoulders)

$+$ Chemical reaction (dark swelling soil, exhausted air made live again, rocks red and blue and ocher, life, dreams, death and rebirth and all bright hopes)

EQUALS

This our world, and behold, she is very fair.

Nevertheless there was a weariness and desolation in the man, and after a while he turned for comfort as if the woman had been his.

"Easy," he said, and the word and his tones meant: (It was too easy, for us and for them. They had a holy spirit, those men. It should have ended otherwise. Fire and fury, wrath, destruction, and the unconquerable pride of man against the gods.)

"No," she replied. "This way was better." Quietly,

153

calmly: (Mercy and understanding. We're not wild animals any more, to bare our teeth at the fates.)

Yes. That is the future. Forget all red glories.

"But what is our tomorrow?" he asked. (We stand with the wreckage of a world about our feet, looking into a hollow universe, and we must fill it ourselves. There is no one to help us.)

"Unless there is a destiny," (God, fate, human courage) she said.

"Perhaps there is," he mused. "Consciously or not, a universe has been given into our hands."

She fled from the knowledge, knowing that to answer her he would have to summon up the bravery he needed. Have we the right to take it? If we make ourselves guardians of planets, is that better than Grunewald—blindness of causality, senseless cruelty of chance, the querning in his poor mad head?)

"It would not be thus that we would enter on our destiny," he told her. "We would be unseen, unknown guides, guardians of freedom, not imposers of an arbitrary will. When our new civilization is built, that may be the only work worthy of its hands."

O most glorious destiny! Why should I feel sorrow on this night? And yet there are tears behind my eyes.

She said what had to be said: "Sheila was discharged a few days ago." *I weep for you, my darling in darkness.*

"Yes," he nodded. "I saw it." (She ran out like a little girl. She held her hands up to the sun and laughed.)

"She has found her own answer. You still have to find yours."

His mind worried the past like a dog with a bone. "She didn't know I was watching her." *It was a cold bright morning. A red maple leaf fluttered down and caught in her hair. She used to wear flowers in her hair for me.* "She has already begun to forget me."

"You told Kearnes to help her forget," she said. "That was the bravest thing you ever did. It takes courage to be kind. But are you now strong enough to be kind to yourself?"

"No," he answered. "I don't want to stop loving her. I'm sorry, Helga."

"Sheila will be watched over," she said. "She will not know it, but the Observers will guide her wandering. There is a promising moron colony——" *Anguish* "—north of the city. We have been helping it lately without its knowing. Its leader is a good man, a strong and gentle man. Sheila's blood will be a leaven in their race."

He said nothing.

"Pete," she challenged him, "now you must help yourself."

"No," he said. "But you can change too, Helga. You can will yourself away from me."

"Not when you need me, and know it, and still cling blind to a dead symbol," she replied. "Pete, it is you now who are afraid to face life."

There was a long stillness, only the sea and the wind had voice. The moon was sinking low, its radiance filled their eyes, and the man turned his face from it. Then he shuddered and straightened his shoulders.

"Help me!" he said, and took her hands. "I cannot do it alone. Help me, Helga."

There are no words. There can never be words for this.

The minds met, flowing together, succoring need, and in a way which was new to the world they shared their strength and fought free of what was past.

To love, honor, and cherish, until death do us part.

It was an old story, she thought among the thunders. It was the oldest and finest story on Earth, so it was entitled to an old language. Sea, and stars—why, there was even a full moon.

CHAPTER *21*

AUTUMN again, and winter in the air. The fallen leaves lay in heaps under the bare dark trees and hissed and rattled across the ground with every wind. Only a few splashes of color remained in the woods, yellow or bronze or scarlet against grayness.

Overhead the wild geese passed in great flocks, southward bound. There was more life in the sky this year—fewer hunters, Brock supposed. The remote honking drifted down to him, full of wandering and loneliness. It was a clear pale blue up there, the sun wheeled bright and heatless, spilling its coruscant light across a broad and empty land. The wind was strong, flowing around his cheeks and flapping his clothes, the trees were noisy with it.

He went slowly from the main house, scuffing the sere grass under his boots. Joe followed quietly at heel. From the shed came a hammering of sheet iron, Mehitabel and Mac were building their charcoal gas distillator: for them it was too much fun to let be, and the gasoline supplies were very low. Some of the people had gone to town, some were sleeping off their Sunday dinner. Brock was alone.

He thought he might stop in and chatter with Mehitabel. No, let her work undisturbed; her conversation was rather limited anyway. He decided to take a stroll through the woods; it was late afternoon already, and too nice a day to be indoors.

Ella Mae came out of one of the cottages and giggled at him. "Hello," she said.

"Uh, hello," he answered. "How're you?"

"I'm fine," she said. "Want to come inside? Nobody else in here now."

"No, thanks," he said. "I, well, I have to check a fence."

"I could come along?" she asked timidly.

"Better not," he said. "The pigs, you know. They might still be running around in there."

Ella Mae's watery blue eyes filled with tears, and she lowered her misshapen head. "You never stop by with me," she accused.

"I will when I get the chance," he said hastily. "It's just that I'm awful busy. You know how it goes." He made his retreat as fast as he could.

Have to get a husband for her, he reflected. *There must be a number of her kind wandering loose even now. I can't have her chasing after me this way, it's too hard on both of us.*

He grinned crookedly. Leadership seemed to be all burden and little reward. He was commander, planner, executive, teacher, doctor, father confessor—and now matchmaker!

He bent over and caressed Joe's head with a big rough hand. The dog licked his wrist and wagged a joyous tail. Sometimes a man could get damnably lonely. Even a friend like Joe couldn't fill all needs. On this day of wind and sharp light and blowing leaves, a day of farewell, when all the earth seemed to be breaking up its summer home and departing down some unknown road, he felt his own isolation like a pain within him.

Now, no more of such thoughts, he reproved himself. "Come on, Joe, let's take us a walk."

The dog poised, it was a lovely taut stance, and looked toward the sky. Brock's eyes followed. The flash of metal was so bright it hurt him to look.

An airship—some kind of airship. And it's landing!

He stood with his fists clenched at his sides, feeling the wind chill on his skin and hearing how it roared in the branches behind him. The heart in his breast seemed absurdly big, and he shivered under the heavy jacket and felt sweat on his palms.

Take it easy, he told himself. *Just take it easy. All right, so it is one of Them. He won't bite you. Nobody's harmed us, or interfered with us, yet.*

Quietly as a falling leaf, the vessel grounded nearby. It was a small ovoid, with a lilting grace in its clean lines and curves, and there was no means of propulsion that Brock could see. He began walking toward it, slowly and stiffly. The revolver sagging at his waist made him feel ridiculous, as if he had been caught in a child's playsuit.

He felt a sudden upsurge of bitterness. *Let Them take us as we are. Be damned if I'll put on company manners for some bloody Sunday tourist.*

The side of the aircraft shimmered and a man stepped through it. *Through it!* Brock's first reaction was almost disappointment. The man looked so utterly commonplace. He was of medium height, a stockiness turning plump, an undistinguished face, an ordinary tweed sports outfit. As Brock approached, the man smiled.

"How do you do?"

"How do." Brock stopped, shuffling his feet and looking

157

at the ground. Joe sensed his master's unease and snarled, ever so faintly.

The stranger held out his hand. "My name is Lewis, Nat Lewis from New York. Hope you'll pardon this intrusion. John Rossman sent me up. He's not feeling very well or he'd have come himself."

Brock shook hands, a little reassured by Rossman's name. The old man had always been a decent sort, and Lewis' manner was ingratiating. Brock forced himself to meet the other man's eyes, and gave his own name.

"Yes, I recognize you from Rossman's description," said Lewis. "He's quite interested in how you people are making out up here. Don't worry, he has no intention of repossessing this property; it's just a friendly curiosity. I work at his Institute, and frankly, I was curious myself, so I've come to check up for him."

Brock decided that he liked Lewis. The man spoke rather slowly, it must be a slight effort for him to return to old ways of speech, but there was nothing patronizing about him.

"From what I hear, you've done a marvelous job," said Lewis.

"I didn't know that you—well—that we——" Brock halted, stammering.

"Oh, yes, a bit of an eye was kept on you as soon as we'd taken care of our own troubles. Which were plenty, believe me. Still are, for that matter. Here, may I offer you a cigar?"

"Hmmm—well——" Brock accepted but didn't smoke it. He had not formed the habit. But he could give the cigar to someone else. "Thanks."

"It's not a baby," Lewis grinned. "At least, I hope not!" He lit one for himself, using a trick lighter that worked even in the high, noisy wind.

"You've doubtless noticed that the towns around here have all been evacuated," he said after taking a contented puff.

"Yes, for some months now," answered Brock. With defiance: "We've been taking what we needed and could find there."

"Oh, quite all right. That was the idea; in fact, you can

158

move into any of them if you want. The colony committee just thought it was best to rid you of such, ah, overwhelming neighbors. The people didn't care; at the present stage of their development, one place is about as good as another to them." Wistfulness flitted across Lewis' face. "That's a loss of ours: the intimacy of giving our hearts to one small corner of the earth."

The confession of weakness relaxed Brock. He suspected that it was deliberate, but even so——

"And those who've strayed here to join you have often been unobtrusively guided," Lewis went on. "There will be others, if you want them. And I think you could use more help, and they could certainly use a home and security."

"It's—nice of you," said Brock slowly.

"Ah, it isn't much. Don't think you've been guarded against all danger, or that all your work was done for you. That was never true, and never will be. We've just—well, once in a while we've thrown a little opportunity your way. But it was up to you to use it."

"I see."

"We can't help you more than that. Too much for us to do, and too few of us to do it. And our ways are too different. Your kind and my kind have come to the parting of the roads, Brock, but we can at least say goodby and shake hands."

It was a warming speech, something thawed inside Brock and he smiled. He had not relished the prospect of being stamped out by a ruthless race of gods, and still less had he cared to spend his days as anyone's ward. Lewis made no bones about the fact of their difference, but he was not snobbish about it either: there was no connotation of superiority in what he said.

They had been strolling about the grounds as they talked. Lewis heard the clashing hammers inside the shed now, and glanced questioningly at Brock.

"I've got a chimpanzee and a moron in there, making a charcoal apparatus so we can fuel our engines," Brock explained. It didn't hurt to say "moron"—not any more. "It's our day off here, but they insisted on working anyway."

159

"How many have you got, all told?"

"Oh, well, ten men and six women, ages from around fifteen to—well, I'd guess sixty for the oldest. Mentally from imbecile to moron. Then a couple of kids have been born too. Of course, it's hard to say where the people leave off and the animals begin. The apes, or Joe here, are certainly more intelligent and useful than the imbeciles." Joe wagged his tail and looked pleased. "I draw no distinctions; everyone does what he's best fitted for, and we share alike."

"You're in command, then?"

"I suppose so. They always look to me for guidance. I'm not the brightest one of the lot, but our two intellectuals are—well—ineffectual."

Lewis nodded. "It's often that way. Sheer intelligence counts for less than personality, strength of character, or the simple ability to make decisions and stick by them." He looked sharply at his bigger companion. "You're a born leader, you know."

"I am? I've just muddled along as well as possible."

"Well," chuckled Lewis, "I'd say that was the essence of leadership."

He looked around the buildings and out to the wide horizon. "It's a happy little community you've built up," he said.

"No," answered Brock frankly. "It's not."

Lewis glanced at him, raising his eyebrows, but said nothing.

"We're too close to reality here for snugness," said Brock. "That may come later, when we're better adjusted, but right now it's still hard work keeping alive. We have to learn to live with some rather harsh facts of life—such as some of us being deformed, or the need for butchering those poor animals——" He paused, noticed that his fists were clenched, and tried to ease himself with a smile.

"Are you—married?" inquired Lewis. "Pardon my nosiness, but I have a reason for asking."

"No. I can't see taking what's available here. No matter, there's enough to do to keep me out of mischief."

"I see——"

Lewis was quiet for a while. They had wandered over

by the corn crib, where a board across two barrels made a seat out of the wind. They sat down, wordlessly, and let the day bluster around them. Joe flopped at their feet, watching them with alert brown eyes.

Presently Lewis stubbed out his cigar and spoke again. He sat looking ahead of him, not facing Brock, and his voice sounded a little dreamy, as if he were talking to himself.

"You and your animals here are making the best of a new situation," he said. "So far it's not been a very good one. Would you want to return to the old days?"

"Not I, no," said Brock.

"I thought not. You're taking this reality which has been given to you, with all its infinite possibilities, and you're making it good. That's what my branch of the race is also trying to do, Brock, and maybe you'll succeed better than we. I don't know. I probably won't ever know—won't live that long.

"But I want to tell you something. I've been out in space—between the stars—and there have been other expeditions there too. We found that the galaxy is full of life, and all of it seems to be like the old life of Earth: many forms, many civilizations, but nowhere a creature like man. The average I.Q. of the whole universe may not be much over a hundred. It's too early to tell, but we have reasons to think that that is so.

"And what are we, the so-called normal humanity, to do with our strange powers? Where can we find something that will try and challenge us, something big enough to make us humble and offer us a task in which we can take pride? I think the stars are our answer. Oh, I don't mean we intend to establish a galactic empire. Conquest is a childishness we've laid aside, even now. Nor do I mean that we'll become ministering angels to all these uncounted worlds, guiding them and guarding them till their races get too flabby to stand on their own feet. No, nothing like that. We'll be creating our own new civilization, one which will spread between the stars, and it will have its own internal goals, creation, struggle, hope—the environment of man is still primarily man.

"But I think there will be a purpose in that civilization
161

For the first time, man will really be going somewhere; and I think that his new purpose will, over thousands and millions of years, embrace all life in the attainable universe. I think a final harmony will be achieved such as no one can now imagine.

"We will not be gods, or even guides. But we will—some of us—be givers of opportunity. We will see that evil does not flourish too strongly, and that hope and chance happen when they are most needed, to all those millions of sentient creatures who live and love and fight and laugh and weep and die, just as man once did. No, we will not be embodied Fate; but perhaps we can be Luck. And even, it may be, Love."

The man smiled then, a very human smile at himself and all his own pretences. "Never mind. I talk too much. Winelike autumn air, as the old cliché has it." He turned to Brock. "What's more to the point, we—our sort—are not going to remain here on Earth."

Brock nodded silently. The vision before him was too enormous for surprise.

"Your sort won't be bothered," said Lewis. "And then in a few years, when things are ready, we'll disappear into the sky. Earth will be left to your kind, and to the animals. And thereafter you will be altogether free. It will be up to you, as to the other kinds of life, to work out your own destiny. And if now and then a bit of luck comes to you— well, that has always been happening."

"Thank you." It was a whisper in Brock's throat.

"Don't thank me, or anyone else. This is merely the logic of events working itself out. But I wish you well, every one of you."

Lewis stood up and began walking back toward his aircraft. "I have to go now." He paused. "I wasn't quite honest with you when I came. It wasn't Rossman's curiosity that sent me; he could have satisfied that by asking the colony committee, or by dropping in himself. I wanted to check up here personally because—well, you'll be having a new member for your community soon."

Brock looked at him, wondering. Lewis stopped before his craft.

"She's an old friend," he said. "Her story is rather tragic, she'll tell you herself when she feels like it. But she's a good sort, a wonderful girl really, and we who know her want her to be happy."

The metal shimmered before him. He took Brock's hand. "Good-by," he said simply, and stepped inside. A moment later his vessel was high in heaven.

Brock stared after it till it had vanished.

When he turned back toward the house, the sun was sinking low and the chill bit at him. They'd have to light the fireplace tonight. Maybe they could break out some of the remaining ale if a new recruit was coming, and Jimmy could play the guitar while they all sang. The songs were rowdy, you couldn't expect more of a pioneer people, but there was warmth in them, steadfastness and comradeship.

He saw her then, walking up the driveway, and his heart stumbled within him. She was not tall, but her form was sweet and strong under the heavy clothing, and bronze-colored hair blew around a face that was young and gentle and good to look on. She carried a bundle on her back, and the suns of many days tramping down open roads had tinged her and dusted freckles across the large-eyed face. He stood for a moment without stirring, and then he ran; but when he came up and was before her, he could find no words.

"Hello," she said shyly.

He nodded awkwardly. It did not occur to him that he was a strong-looking man, not handsome, but with something about him that invoked trust.

"I heard talk this was a refuge," she said.

"Yes," he replied. "Have you come far?"

"From New York City." There was a small shiver in her, and he wondered what had happened there. Or maybe it was just the cold. The wind piped bitterly now. "My name is Sheila," she said.

"I'm Archie—Archie Brock." Her hand was firm within his. She did not act frightened, and he knew that while she might not be quite as smart as he, she had more than enough intelligence and will to meet this wintering planet. "You're welcome here. It's always a big event when someone new comes. But you'll find it strange, and we all have to work hard."

"I'm not afraid of either of those," she answered. "I don't think I can ever be afraid again."

He took her bundle and started back. The western sky was turning red and gold and a thin chill green. "I'm glad to know you, Miss—what did you say your last name was?"

"Sheila," she replied. "Just Sheila."

They walked up the driveway side by side, the dog and the wind at their heels, toward the house. In there was shelter.

About Poul Anderson

What would happen if

Those are magic words, and the writer who chooses to follow out their intention finds himself suddenly released in a world unbounded by *here and now* and open to the farthest reaches of logic and imagination. What would happen if philosophers were kings, if men could live forever, if the human race could suddenly surmount the limits of its present intelligence?

Such a train of thought has been the starting point for some of the most fascinating works of imaginative fiction, and it is to this class of informed speculation that BRAIN WAVE belongs. Poul Anderson (the pronunciation lies midway between "pole" and "powl") is, like many of the best writers in science fiction, a graduate physicist. (The physical sciences seem to be producing as many authors as medicine did a generation ago.) As such, he brings to fiction that sense of the possible that the widening horizon of science often bestows.

"I was born in Bristol, Pennsylvania, in 1926," he writes, "but did not get around to science fiction until 1937. I was rather snobbishly determined not to read such awful pulp, but fell sick and had nothing else to do—and thereafter I was hooked.

"At the University of Minnesota, I majored in physics, graduating with honors in 1948. But apart from a little assisting here and there, I have not worked in the field. What happened was that writing, which had been a hobby for a long time, began to pay off while I was in college with some sales to *Astounding Science Fiction*. I decided to take a year off, living by the typewriter, and the year has been extended ever since.

"I don't intend to make science fiction an exclusive career —I've already done a bit of historical writing and am planning some 'serious' novels—but within its limits, it is a fascinating line of work. It permits a long view of the future, a chance to play with ideas, to study the workings of man, to show the consequences of theory in action."

DEL REY *The brightest Science Fiction stars in the galaxy!*

Catch a Rising Star!

DEL REY

Jack L. Chalker

A JUNGLE OF STARS	25457	1.50
THE WEB OF THE CHOZEN	27376	1.75
MIDNIGHT AT THE WELL OF SOULS	25768	1.95
DANCERS IN THE AFTERGLOW	27564	1.75

James P. Hogan

INHERIT THE STARS	25704	1.50
THE GENESIS MACHINE	27231	1.75
THE GENTLE GIANTS OF GANYMEDE	27375	1.75

Tony Rothman

THE WORLD IS ROUND	27213	1.95

LG-5

DEL REY *SCIENCE FICTION CLASSICS FROM BALLANTINE BOOKS*

CHILDHOOD'S END, Arthur C. Clarke	27603	1.95
FAHRENHEIT 451, Ray Bradbury	27431	1.95
HAVE SPACESUIT, WILL TRAVEL, Robert A. Heinlein	26071	1.75
IMPERIAL EARTH, Arthur C. Clarke	25352	1.95
MORE THAN HUMAN, Theodore Sturgeon	24389	1.50
RENDEZVOUS WITH RAMA, Arthur C. Clarke	27344	1.95
RINGWORLD, Larry Niven	27550	1.95
A SCANNER DARKLY, Philip K. Dick	26064	1.95
SPLINTER OF THE MIND'S EYE, Alan Dean Foster	26062	1.95
STAND ON ZANZIBAR, John Brunner	25486	1.95
STAR WARS, George Lucas	26079	1.95
STARMAN JONES, Robert A. Heinlein	27595	1.75
TUNNEL IN THE SKY, Robert A. Heinlein	26065	1.50
UNDER PRESSURE, Frank Herbert	27540	1.75